The Divine Symphony

Books by
Calvin Miller
FROM BETHANY HOUSE PUBLISHERS

The Divine Symphony

Into the Depths of God

Snow

The Unchained Soul

Wind

CALVIN MILLER

The Divine Symphony

BETHANY HOUSE PUBLISHERS
MINNEAPOLIS, MINNESOTA 55438

The Divine Symphony
Copyright © 1989, 1990, 2000
Calvin Miller

Originally published in two volumes, entitled *A Requiem for Love*
and *A Symphony in Sand* by Word Publishing.

Cover illustrations, except violin, by T. M. Williams
Cover design by Jennifer Parker
Interior illustrations by Rick Wipple

Published by Bethany House Publishers
A Ministry of Bethany Fellowship International
11400 Hampshire Avenue South
Minneapolis, Minnesota 55438
www.bethanyhouse.com

Printed in the United States of America by
Bethany Press International, Minneapolis, Minnesota 55438

Library of Congress Cataloging-in-Publication Data

Miller, Calvin.
    [Requiem for love]
    The divine symphony / by Calvin Miller.
       p. cm.
Previously published as: A requiem for love. c1989; and, A
symphony in sand. c1990.
    ISBN 0-7642-2170-1
    1. Mary, Blessed Virgin, Saint—Fiction. 2. Christian women
saints—Palestine—Fiction. 3. Creation—Fiction. I. Miller,
Calvin. Symphony in sand. II. Title: Symphony in sand.
III. Title.
PS3563.I376 D58 2000
813'.54—dc21
                                       00-008166

A REQUIEM FOR LOVE

No serpent ever crawled so low
He did not dream of thrones and
crowns.

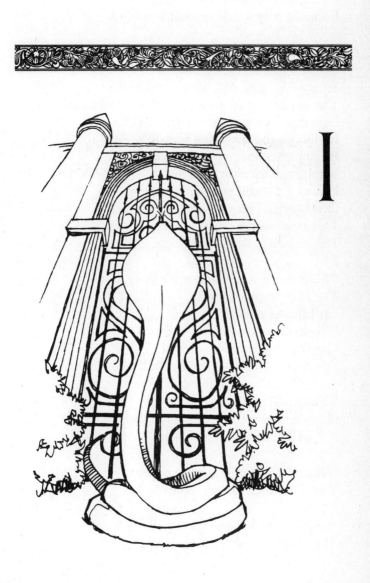

I

He came like loving wind
And left the sand astir behind Him.
The desert burned in early sun
As He approached the towering gates,
Knowing they would open at His word.

He knew His hissing foe would be there,
Brilliant gold and scarlet evil,
Yellow-eyed with old, diminished hope.
The serpent spoke, rising from his coiled form,
Straining for a glimpse inside the gates.
He longed to know what wonders
His almighty enemy was fashioning
Beyond the boundaries of evil.
He saw . . . and yet saw nothing.
One hurried blur of shimmering greens
That mocked the starving sands
The serpent called his kingdom.

"Welcome to your Garden, Eminence,"
The rising reptile hissed.
Earthmaker turned,
"Slithe, once-loved, once crowned
Can this be you,
Self-damned, condemned to sand?"

Slithe laughed.
"Lock me from the green; it is only for a while.
Full well you know, I *will* be in."

"Once the entire universe was yours.
You chose these desert chains."

"I chose a throne and got the chains,"
The serpent spewed his bitter grudge.

The Father-Spirit turned toward the gates
As they swung slowly open.
His old accuser blinked into the distant splendor.
"Will You succeed this time
In fashioning a lover
Who will remain a lover?
Or, is Your new creation
Destined to betray You?
Why are You forever
Planting hope in high-walled gardens?"

The Father-Spirit looked away.
"Terra holds this Sanctuary as a dream
Where love abused by treachery
May mold a masterpiece of hope.
Today I crown all I have ever made
And honor Terra's clay by stamping it *Imago Mei*,
A man, a prince—Regis, friend of spirit.
He shall wear the crown of love you cast aside.
But you shall never see his coronation,
For only perfect love shall pass these gates."

"Has this new creature, gift of choice?
Can this Regis, Prince of Terra,
Bid me enter, or is he just a puppet
Stringed hand and foot to Your almighty fingers?
Does he dance to Your enslaving orders,
Obeying You, daring nothing on his own?
Obey . . . Now there's a word for you. . .
Obey . . . A scab on freedom . . . A collar and
       a chain,
An insult to all dignity. Will you tell him
As you call him into life,
'Obey Me, Regis, and I'll love you
But if you're naughty, out you go!'
Has he will, I ask You?"

The Father-Spirit smiled.
The huge gates swung fully open now, exposing
   Sanctuary.
"Behold, low Serpent-King, what you can never
   have . . .
I'm going in now. This day is triumph
For the Masterpiece is done!
And I will soon en-spirit him with being.
Man shall be born and stand a king today!"

"He shall be Regis, lover of his Maker.
Man made to cherish truth, and bless the morning
   sun—
Valor with a dream, bold to excise evil—
Chaste love and high compassion,
Heaping dignity on all he touches!
Man shall devote himself to beauty and to art.
Knowledge will be treasure unto him
Giving birth to science.
And with science he shall widen all this shining
   place
Till My garden claims your barren realm."

Made miserable by all he'd lost,
The serpent spat out venom.
"Your dream is proof of error!"
"Almighty in naïveté is what You are.
Go ahead . . . .
Close these gates that shut out nothing!
If Regis has the slightest will,
I'll smash his chain and set him free.
And Your weak and foolish Prince
Will give his crown, at last, to me!
Will You never learn, Earthmaker?
There are no walled retreats—
No soul that does not yearn
To know the sweet forbidden.
The freedom that You always give

Becomes at last the very weapon
That we level at Your heart."·

Slithe slithered close to the grand gates.
With the desert at his back, he sang
A haunting chant of despair.

"He is born today . . . man who comes to nothing!
His bloody soul will murder peace
And he shall mine the earth for swords and spears
Till Earthmaker's noble dreams lie still
In rotting battlefields.
Man, the grisly joke Earthmaker plays upon Himself.
Man, the vicious image of his Maker,
Blinding birds to make them sing,
Chaining kindred men to make them slaves,
Gouging Terra's fields with avarice,
Burying himself in bulging-eyed excesses.

Great Earthmaker, must I tell You what You know?
Man will not follow truth nor worship art,
He will follow what his greed shall nominate,
Leave his children begging life from wolves.
Crown his appetites till gluttony is queen
And lust is king, ruling
His degenerate kingdom from a soiled bed.
Today, when You en-spirit him with life
And make him free to choose,
You dare not tell him that
There is a Serpent in the desert.
For if man knows that I exist,
His appetite to have all that is forbidden
Will splinter these tall gates, crying out to evil,
'Come in, O come . . . I've learned too narrowly!'
I've only then to sleep, and when I wake
Your eagle will leave sky to be a snake."

The gates clanged shut.

Life found itself alive
And somehow knew its opposite was
    death.
We are ever being born, or dying,
And the thrill of choosing is
    ours.
Only once, must we be born without
    our own consent.
Only once, must we die without our
    own permission.

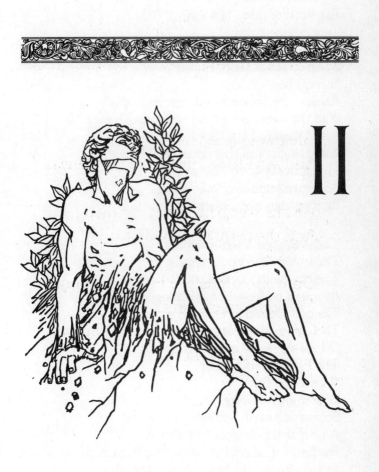

II

Inside the high, closed gates
The Father-Spirit walked,
Silent in the leafy temples
Of man's birthing altar.
Earthmaker made His way
To a sylvan grotto
Where His sleeping sculpture waited.
Spirit stared at flesh, exulting!
"Live, Man!
Receive the breath to call me 'Father'!
And the sweetness of the name shall honor Me.
And I shall call you 'Son'—
And the glory of that name shall honor you.
I breathe My spirit into you
As benediction over manhood.
Be sovereign over Sanctuary!"

The eyes grew bright with life,
The noble head raised regally.
The dry earth cracked and fell away,
As music broke—like lightning, and
Thunder pealed in Spirit-laughter.
The clay-made creature stood!
"Move and grow in understanding."
The Father-Spirit spoke.
"I give you Terra
Glistening in sunlight.
Stones and earth and mist,
A pool that calls your face a twin.
Feather, fur, and fang—claw, and fingernail.
Sky, distance, leaf, blade, green, and blue."

The new prince studied his new world,
And staring at all that was made,
He saw the great unseeable.
His emotions reached,

Growing, swelling as he realized
He was in love not with what was merely made,
But with the lavish Maker of so rich a world.
"Spirit, intangible! I am wrapped in new passion
Lost in first-being.
Here upon this planet I have found myself alive,
And best of all the friend of Earthmaker.
Father-Spirit, I am made today nobility, high-born,
Crowned rich with Grace!
I LOVE YOU!"

"Father, Maker of myself,
I join these gentle zephyrs
That stir the ferns to praise!
I bless the creature eyes that peer
Through forest walls.
Listen now, glad heart,
To swirling wingbeats.
See the silver fire that leaps from fin
To mirrored lake
And sleeps in shimmering promises.

The naked Prince laid down in the grass
Soaking life from Terra's ochre soil.
"Son!" Earthmaker breathed the gallant word,
Soft and often as the breeze that
Whispered oaks alive.
"Gift unto Myself—
The Prince of presence—
Lest I should ever be alone.
Now, Regis, image of My Being,
You are the Child
To brighten My lonely house
And the glad resolution to My years inside Myself."

The new man listened, overcome by Presence.
To be given all the world at once,
Stopped his tongue

And left his wit too dead for words.
Overwhelmed, he broke the awesome quiet.
"Father, I receive Your gift of being, but
You have made me *too* rich
To name my wealth
And yet too poor
To give You anything of meaning.
I love with only giftless love."

"Regis, there is no such thing as 'giftless' love.
The very words accuse each other.
My gift to you is love, but
Worship is your gift to Me.
And Oh, most glorious it is!
Worship always calls Me 'Father' and
Makes us both rich with a common joy.
Worship Me, for only this great gift
Can set you free from the killing love of self,
And prick your fear with valiant courage
To fly in hope through moments of despair.
Worship will remind you
That no man knows completeness in himself.
Worship will teach you to speak your name,
When you've forgotten who you are.
Worship is duty and privilege,
Debt and grand inheritance at once.
Worship, therefore, at those midnights
When the stars hide.
Worship in the storms till love
Makes thunder whimper and grow quiet
And listen to your whispered hymns.
Worship and be free."
A sparrow darted in between them
Its brown-gold flash of feathers
Stopped in the Father-Spirit's hand.

"Here," said Earthmaker, "is your sister.
Life not so high as yours—

Nor yet aware of its own separate self,
But sacred!"

Regis took the bird.
And held it in his hand,
Stroked it and released it.
It flew away.

"Tell me all of life and love,"
The Earth-born Regent pled.

"In time . . . In time.
For now, let life and love be one.
As I have ever been . . ."

"But I have not . . ."

"Deny not, Regis, how long you've lived.
In the misty, deep and unmarked
Crevasses of time, you have always lived
In the very vastness of My heart
As the waiting portrait of My eternal being."

The Spirit and His shining creature,
Encircled hearts and drew themselves to
            union . . .
Being in embrace . . . Creature and Creator
So in love that the sky and breeze declared it!
"Father, is love forever?"

"It may be, son . . . It may be!
Only worship Me, and you shall see
That love will name itself infinity!"

To be touched tells man that he is
    loved.
To touch tells man that he is lover.
Touching is therefore, being
Tango ergo sum!
I touch; therefore, I am!

III

The Father-Spirit was not there
When the crimson morning came
And His absence filled
His waking son with restless emptiness.
For one bright day and spangled night,
His lover did not come.
Regis' heart was set in quest.
By day and night he looked
But neither sun nor moon would speak
Nor disclose the hiding place of God.
"Father!" he called and reached
Up to the thin blue of pale day.
There was no answer.
The sky did not brighten,
The breeze whispered nothing!
"Father, Father . . . . " he called once more.
The quiet grew with greater absence.
"Your world is here, but where are You?
Speak . . . O speak . . . for if You are not here,
Mere created beauty is throatless and purpose deaf.
Where are You, Father?
I have searched the emptiness
And cried out to the mocking stars,
'Where is Love, if He is not?'"

An immediate longing that he could not stem
Washed over him and left him feeling more alone.
His solitary oneness was rebuked by nature's
        "two-ness."
Two doves, white as first light, fluttered past him.
Two deer drank from a nearby pool.
The stag and doe were different
And yet they walked together
In complementing oneness—
So with the cock and hen,
The bruin and his mate.

"All life in Sanctuary comes in twos but mine.
I alone walk in solitude."
Regis' oneness stained his joy with doubt.

In the passing of the days,
Regis often woke entangled in the issue
Of his oneness.
He felt empty—separated
Somehow from all that lived—
Needing something so elusive
It would not define itself!

Yet, if no mate, he had a Father.
Suddenly he felt ashamed because he felt alone
And then he felt alone because he felt ashamed.
Each time he put it from his mind, to think of it
     no more,
The stag and doe would pass again,
And their "two-ness" woke his yearning solitude.

Once wading in a mirrored pool
He suddenly stood still.
Staring down at his reflection.
He cried out to his inner soul,
"If I step from this pool
I'll be alone again."
When Regis knelt to bring his image near
Just the moving of his body
Wrinkled water and cut his face
Into a hurried set of silver ribbons.
He left the pool at last,
Certain that the water's mimicry
Only scoffed at his need.

"O Father-Spirit, come,"
He begged, "Come, Come . . .
I am lonely . . . it is not good.
For loneliness grieves, in starving solitude,

Desperate for stars to talk.
Loneliness is wandering in want,
Making richness poor,
And rendering earth's music tuneless.
Loneliness leaves dancing bound in melancholy."
His words died in empty wind.
An eagle, in the cold sky, screamed!
And Regis stared into the deep abyss
Of despairing oneness,
And for the first time formed
The dark words, "Who am I?"

Hearing the ache in Regis' soul,
The Father-Spirit came at last.

"Consort to Myself,
Reflection of My glory
Are we not two?"

"Not two, but one. I am alone.
Where were You, Father?
I needed You . . ." Regis wept.

"Here! Wherever your eye fell, I was!"

"I couldn't see You . . . You didn't speak!"

"I am here, always . . . In looking for Me, you but
    looked through me.
I spoke a thousand times . . . Did you not hear
    the eagle scream?
The rumbling of the waterfalls?
The songs of nightingales
And clarions of wild rams?"

"How can I know You when You hide,
For even if You speak and hang transparent in the air
Spirit cannot reach with fingers

Firm enough to touch.
Nothing in my world embraces me with nearness.
In my aloneness I find the forest far too wide—
The world too open."

A finch darted to a small nest
And with her feathered mate
Snuggled into tightness.
"See how all the creatures, each one touch
And draw themselves to glorious
Togetherness . . . and life . . . "

"No, Regis,
See the glory that we are!
These creatures are but gentle celebrants of power.
Their tiny glory applauds My creativity
And yet they cannot frame
The smaller meaning that is theirs.
You alone are King of all that I have made,
And Kings wear being as the heavy crown of
        self-awareness.
To be troubled over who you are
Is glory more unspeakable
Than these small creatures can conceive.
It is not their hearts
Only their wingbeats that praise,
'Earthmaker is!'"

"Why then," Regis began,
"Do I yearn to see the open world
Close tighter all around me?"

"Come, Son, despair no more!"
His gentle Father led him
To a grotto altar, edged by thick, concealing ferns.
There, in terra cotta
Lay a silent form begging life.
"Here is she who shall

Complete your need."
Regis bowed his head.
Her beauty reached inward and stirred
A kind of reverence he had never felt before.
She seemed alive, asleep,
About to rise.
He studied the softness in her face,
Her eyes were closed, and yet he sensed
That they were windows waiting to be opened
        unto life.
His eyes fell on her waiting hands
Promising touch.
Suddenly he loved! The emotion flew at him!
He felt it from the inside moving outward,
Rising with power and soul need.
"Father," he breathed,
And his breath was nearly prayer.
"This is my need, beckoning me to nearer
        worship—
At last, a love that touches flesh with flesh!
Let her lie no longer
Begging breath and pulse!"
He paused reflectively, then asked,
"Why only now have You shown this perfect answer
To my emptiness?"

"I gave you yearning oneness
To define your need.
In your hungering to be touched
You found out who you were."

Regis reached out to the clay-dead form.
"Oh, bid her live for me
As lionness to lion,
As stag to doe,
As sire to dame,
As intimacy and all of hope."

"I will . . . but Son . . . first gaze in wonder,
And study all she is—
Dim time beyond the light of vision
Will teach all later ages her full worth!
She is woman, *Gloriana*
In excellence created.
See the face of love!

"Behold her!
Woman, being from man's side.
Liberated from harsh manliness,
Given wisdom unto motherhood,
Tenderness, for her calling as a wife . . .
Music for the lullabies that shall teach her little
        ones to sleep with courage . . .
Strength for lonely widowhood, if life should
        brutalize.
Her power will be in seeing all your fast moving
        eyes shall miss.
She will feel the pain you hurry past.
She will move in gentle inwardness, that sees
        so often
Past your logic-driven days.
Call her 'Woman'!
Give her honor!
Lift her up,
And she will grow secure,
And protected by your affirmation,
She will school you in self worth!"

"Behold and reach!
Touch the sunlight on her hair,
For hair is woman's glory,
Born to you as gold.
These eyes shall look on you with glad esteem,
Bidding love be born.

"Come touch these fragile arms and hands,
Made strong as service,
For she, like you, is made to serve.
These breasts are for the nourishing of life.
Here future sons of yours shall feed.
Here is her body, fertile with possibility.
Rich with power to create life—
Here we three shall one day meet
And the issue from her being shall be glorious.
'Nation' is a word that time will understand
But you and she shall one day make this planet laugh
With continents of children, needing love and
     celebrating joy.
Thus, worshiping Myself, Terra shall know
     purpose."

"Oh, let her live! Give sinew to this clay."
"In time . . . In time . . . ," His Father
     soft-replied,
"My Spirit shall indwell your sleeping bride."

Eden was the birthing room
Of all of modern knowledge.
There darksome sociology was born.
How shall we define
This old, unsettled science?
As homeless Homo Sapiens
Picking apples in the dark
So the orchard owner cannot see.

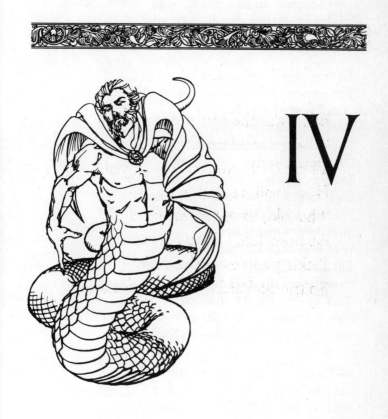

IV

Once again the World Hater
Met Earthmaker near
The gates of Sanctuary.
As before, Earthmaker swirled in spiraled wind
That skittered air and twisted sand toward heaven.
"Today I give them the glorious gift
Of love's full ecstasy," He said.

Through the foaming dust
The serpent glided toward the whirlwind.
"You know where the gift
Of human loving
Will one day take the race.
Dare You trust them with a gift
So easily misgiven, so often uncontrolled?
Such love will only seem their friend.
In truth, it shall rise as pale lust
Bloodless in neural fire
Which shall order them to fury
Till they lie, spent in shallow oneness,
Powerless in the spell of appetites
That fettered them to passion.
Poor creatures . . . children of a devious Father
Who gives them scorpions as gifts!

"A Father whose loving children
Need to touch, but cannot do it
Without summoning destruction—
Think You, that they will worship You,
When their eyes are eager with desire?"

The snake glided to a stone
Already warmed by sunlight.
And the Father-Spirit watched,
As the Serpent changed himself
Into a man.

"See, even I am man enough
To summon fire
And call Prince Regis' bride
To lie with me and widen knowledge.
You know the end of Eros!
Keep human rapture to yourself
Or, at least, don't call it gift!
Give them rather hemlock
And let them die believing that
Human ecstasy is nobler than it is."

"My gifts are ever right," Earthmaker thundered.
"And what I give to both My children
Shall nourish them with close dependence.
This gift is fire, to forge
Their closeness when the night is cold.
Intimacy is its name
And righteousness, its bond.
They will lift it as the treasure
Of their union—
Divinely given flame,
To warm not burn
Nor ever rage in selfishness.
They shall receive this gift in gratitude,
And worship Me for giving it."

"Worship in the midst of lust—Hah!
They shall abuse, not use, this gift.
Their need for You will be swallowed whole
In eager, vulgar hunger."
The Father-Spirit left the desert,
And the shrieking Slithe,
For He would no longer listen to
His blasphemy of human loving.

So stepping into Sanctuary,
The Father whispered wisdom on the breeze.
"My children, Regis and Regina,

Regents of primeval Terra,
I bring you both a gift
That shall endow you with
Strong dreams of love's posterity.
You shall live on through this gift
Eternal in your children,
Eternal in My love!
But . . . beware,
Teach this gift discipline,
Let it never ever feed capriciously
Eating what it will and when.
You must not ever take the gift beyond your union,
Or offer it, uncherished, to any cheaper use.
If it wanders curiously afield,
Remind it of its Giver,
And bid it mind its pure intent.
Two are the keepers of this gift.
For three, it holds obscenity and death.
Be born in splendor and esteem the night,
Your loving shall be king, not appetite."

It is the eye that bids the fingers reach.
It is the touching finger that
Calls its parent-hand to grasp and
    hold.
But, grasping kills all
That the eye at first desired.
So touch is strong narcotic,
Begging lovers to an addiction.

V

Wind twisted into clay,
And the clay received it
As the breath of its Creator.
"Live!" howled the laughing
Gales of life.

The Queen, effused by Spirit,
Rose and gazed, as color
Baptized her sight in splendor.
"Daughter . . . " said the Father,
"Set your feet upon the Earth,
And make it tremble
With the imperial authority
Of first existence.
You are born today,
And bring a double crown to both of us.
Your crown is human being.
My crown is instant Fatherhood.
Live and bless us both."

He thrilled to watch her first steps.
She waved her hands low, sideward,
As though the gentle fanning of the air
Would balance her tremulous uprightness.
Timidly, the woman-child walked,
The loving wind held Spirit-hands
To keep her from falling as she
Straightened then and moved
From fear to purpose,
As learning child to strident Empress
In but a score of steps.

"I love you, Daughter . . .
But linger not so near your birthing altar.
My lonely Son is waiting,
Dreaming of your coming.

Go and offer him
The gift of human loving,
And you shall teach
This living planet Grace!"

She walked as dignity to coronation
While, unknowing, the Prince of Terra waited.

The trees rose stiff and tall, erect, remote.
Regis stood and looked away,
Again alone . . . alone . . . alone.
Till suddenly, beauty seared his vision.
He was like a child who, staring at the sun,
Is blinded by the brilliance.

Across the meadow where the
World fell into tangled green—
He saw her once again,
Only now—she lived—
Earth-molded woman—
Glorious in sunlight!
Making Sanctuary rich!

The woman's shadow fell ahead of her
And drew her forward toward the man.
She must know him and be with him
And yet she walked in measured steps,
For she had only come to be
And while asking who she was
She now must ask who he was, too.
Drawn by her face, he, also,
Walked slow with wider stride,
Afraid a hurried pace would wipe away
The lovely apparition and leave him lonely
        once again.
"Be born at last my vision!
Did ever eye know light till now?"
Breathed Regis and then in wild elation,

He shouted to his living, standing queen,
"Reign with me over earth,
And for your missing throngs of subjects
Take myself—I genuflect before
The royal promise of my Father
Who fills, at last, my need
With such completeness,
I am near to song."

Despairing with a madness given to mirage, they met
At last, like hesitant gazelles in fertile meadows.
They reached with stretching fingertips
Until their threadlike souls were fused
And their joy fell in utter weakness.
Hand gathered fingers into hand.
Eye locked into eye.
They stood while joy rose upward
Through the ground, effusing them with such
        exuberance
Their hypnotic drunkenness must burst
At once in ecstasy!
He turned and so did she.
They ran in glorious two!
Like harts or wildebeests
They fell in laughter in new meadows
And rolled like newborn colts.

"Regis, I am born today along
With love," Regina cried.
"Oh, hold me now as mooring for my spirit
Lest I should rise in rapture
Never more to touch the earth."

Lip brushed eager lip—
Their bodies trembling
In the breeze-kissed forest, touched.
Terra blessed the warmth of

First love.
Closeness folded over in glorious assurance.
And then for reasons which knew no reason—
They broke in gales of running laughter
That joined the frothing melodies of nearby brooks.
The hush of first life gave way
To gentle conversation.
"Are we alone—the two of us?"
Her question answered by the asking,
Slid soundless into waxy leaves,
Dissolved in green, and flew at rising mist.

She pried at his reluctance to break the reverie,
"What did you do before I came?"

"I waited . . . but impatiently," he answered.

"For me?"

"For . . . two . . . for love!"

"And did your Father Spirit not love you?"

"He did and does . . .
You're here because He loves!
I waited and lamented that His
Love was incomplete somehow.
Our Father is all-wise.
He knew exactly what I needed
Before I knew enough to ask."

"Then why did He withhold me
And leave you so alone?"

"Because loneliness is the brooding parent
Of becoming—thought and busy being
Seldom come together.

Regina, He is a gentle lover
Whose glorious love is a gentle teacher.

"And can I meet this Father-Lover?"

"You cannot escape *that* joy!
In every sunrise you will meet Him.
Put any blossom to your ear
And it will whisper love's full name.
You will meet our Father
A thousand times each day you live.
He thrusts Himself as oak to sky.
Hangs out the lights of night
That twinkle to assure us
He is here—As life is here."

"I see Him even now
Within your eyes—
His glory lights your hair.
His warmth is in your touch.
His trust walks in your footprints.
His power calls me to give my body
To your keeping
As He gave you to me.
Ask not if you shall meet Him.
He swims the air we breathe—
Inhabits light.
Unless your eyes should fail
And all your senses die,
You must meet *Him*, who can on any day,
Fashion love from ordinary clay."

A godless pilgrim wandered, searching.
Young, he first sought God among the
    roses;
Old and dim of eye, he looked among
    the stars
And cried with withered, empty hands
That never had held truth,
"Where can I find God?"
The crying wind replied,
"Only at the seam of mud and mystery
Where spirit marries flesh."

VI

S it here," said the Man.
"Lean back against my chest."
He felt her hair like flaxen
Filaments of glory
Fashioned into richness
By the blazing, fading sun.
"By all He is, I love you.
Come Father-Spirit,
Bless our joyous oneness with Your presence."

The Father-Spirit came,
"Children, formed by My own spirit fingers,
I bless you."

"Father?" Regina softly asked.
"Who was Your maker?
What world was Sanctuary unto You?"

Earthmaker pointed outward into space,
As an upward draft of wind
That lifts a floating leaf to sky,
"I come from where
There is no coming—I walked
The pathless paths of unborn universe.
Before I taught the light its radiance.
I knew the night of nothingness
While still it hungered for the warmth of worlds.
Now, you, My children,
Crown My universe with meaning.
You yearn for truth
As cold yearns to be warm,
And dark lusts after light.
Oh, at last, my empty Terra
Knows her dwelling place!"

The three then walked
Until at last they stood between two trees.

Here the Father-Spirit, elusive as a breeze
Spoke into the stillness.
"Between these trees lies great responsibility.
Here you must remember who you are
And treasure our relationship.
Hold to all you honor.
The fruit of these two trees
Shall be your burden.
The fruit of one is morning,
Blessing you with rich unending day.
The fruit of the other is sunset,
Dark with the nectar of destruction.
Eat of morning and bless our love.
Eat of sunset, and you will soon love only
        things.
Then craving power, you will turn from service
And broken trust will devour our oneness.

"Despair not—but remember
All being knows a heaviness of burden.
I, too, must bear a burden.
I took it up when I created you
And made you free to choose.
My children, your Father, too, knows heaviness.
All being bears a weight
Proportioned to its size.
To stride these stars
With all that I must carry,
Would break the spine of spindling galaxies.

"I wanted you to be,
And yet I would not give you
Empty being . . . I made you free to choose,
Aware your choices might
Destroy all.

"To make lovers, who might at any time,
Become the fanged monsters

That spring at love and sting it with a poisonous
     treason,
Is my God-sized burden.

"Implanting love and choice in you
Is that heaviness which I must carry,
Staggering underneath the weight
Of what I've given.
I know at last My children might greet Me
With faithless daggers,
Stabbing Fatherhood—
Not killing it but wounding all its dreams.

"Choose carefully therefore, for,
Between the morning and the sunset of your
     choosing
You may discover
The Hater of this world.
He smashes planets, ruins stars . . .
Gives birth to hell in Heaven's midst.
Eat only for your appetite,
And you shall unleash his destructive evil
In this fair place."

For the first time in her brief, new life,
Naïveté parted like forking water,
And Regina saw choice as utter terror.
When every day held choices to be made,
Every choice was threatening with consequence.
She must choose good so quickly
She'd have no time to choose good's opposite.

"Is the Hater of this world in sanctuary?"
Asked the woman.

"He will be or may be.
The same desire which
Summoned Me will summon him."

"Never shall we summon him,"
Regina was firm . . . "Never"
And yet a twinge of curiosity
Touched her deeply and she wondered if
What she did not know
Was somehow *worth* the knowing.
The sunset smothered her in cold fatigue
As her desires now fondled new intrigue.

Hate never tells the truth convincingly
And Caesar's cry,
Et tu, Bruté,
Is always love
Reaching out to try to understand
Why trust cannot be trusted . . .
Why all our lovers carry daggers,
And why Judas kisses freely only
In Gethsemanes of need.

VII

The Prince of Sanctuary woke each day,
As one whose dreams would not let go of him.
The fullness of his love
Reached out to touch his queen.
To but see her was to want to touch her,
And to touch her, begged him hold her.
Love was so abundant and at hand,
He felt a stinging brightness in his own eyes,
When he but looked at his beloved.

One night within the glade
Where they had drawn
The garlands of their bower
About themselves, Regina asked,
"Is the World-Hater enemy
To all our Father loves?"

The man nodded.
"He is someone in this starry universe
Whom we will never meet."

"Still I am intrigued by all
I do not know of power.
What is power? What is it like?"

"I cannot say
But it lies opposite of our Father's love.
As love is sun, so craving power is ice.
As love creates, power may destroy.
As love makes one . . . power sometimes
        amputates
And divorces lovers by its unholy greed."

"Still," Regina wondered,
"Power, like love, may be a kind of knowing.

Oh, that I knew all that may be known."
Each looked away,
As though her words desired too much.

They said little else as daylight faded
But Regina slept—In restlessness
Stirring in their bower,
Waking only once in darkness
And crying to the night,
"Can love be love
Until it knows its opposite?"
She fell again to troubled sleep.

Regis sensed her discontent
When first light woke them both.
He led her from the glade
Unto the altar where both of them were born.
"Let us, here, where we both woke to light,
Kneel and remember how Almighty-love once
        fashioned our completeness
From the hungers of my solitude."
He paused, then bowed his head
And worshiped with a single word, "Father."
Regina worshiped with a single word . . . "Love."
Their simple act of reverence
Gave way to singing.
"The Father gave the world to us
And woke us with the Light of Love!"

The man then left off his praise,
Too full to speak, made mute by
Double ardor . . .
When his joy-choked voice returned
He spoke to both his Maker and his Queen,
"Twice-loved am I, and made so wealthy,
That I dare not choose which worship I should
        treasure most.

Give counsel every breeze to name priority,
Is love all wealth, and hate all poverty?
My Father's love is sky untouchable.
My woman's fair embrace is earth beneath.
My universe, thus framed with love is light,
Whose radiance is rich, forbidding night!"

Love smiles.
Hate grins.

VIII

Regina left the grotto
Of their worship.
She walked alone
And wondered what it would be like
To actually see
Her Father's enemy.
Her curiosity grew
Until she spoke almost aloud,
"O that I might see him . . ."
Her words were barely out
When she looked and saw,
lying by the water's edge,
A handsome youth—
The only man she'd ever seen
Besides her Prince and Lover.
She blurted out with trembling,
"Are you our enemy?"
Feeling both fear and enticement
She drew instantly away
And yet with reaching curiosity.

He grinned,
Then beckoned with his finger,
"Come, Queen, and know another King.
The wise replace their fear
With broader trust,
And make friends of every terror
That they feel.
I am Slithe, no enemy, but friend.
I'm ready now to serve your curiosity
And answer all your wonder.
There is power, Regina, in the things
That I can teach you.
For evil can be fair as love."
Slithe paused and smiled, then spoke again.
"How well I do remember love,

Simple, plain, single-hearted.
Indeed love once was all I knew
Before I chose to choose.
Your Father-Spirit told me then
That if I widened life past
That thin stingy living
Which He calls obedience,
I would despise
The consequences of my liberty.
But I was forged in freedom's foundry,
And could not live beneath
The thumb of all His threats
And His smothering demands for adoration.
I reached for power!
He slapped my hands!
Still I rose up to grab His scepter,
Telling Him that His tyranny
Was not liberty!
'Rule those content to be the mindless
Serfs of Your enslaving prohibitions!'
I struck at Him with honesty."

Slithe stopped and laughed,
"And then this tyrant you call Father,
Pitched me into space,
Telling me I'd die of disobedience.
But as you clearly see, I didn't.
In fact, I learned a glorious truth that day.
There is a wondrous option to His loving
        narrowness.
For having chosen on my own, I'm free of Him,
With all my visions richer for the choosing.

"He wept, they say, the first day that I hated,
And so, you see, my choosing taught us both."

Regina reached out timidly for logic,
"He bid us trust *Him*, Slithe . . . warning us that

There are things better left unchosen."
"You're not naked," Regina interrupted herself,
"As Prince Regis and myself."
Surprised as much that he was dressed
As that he had ever come to Sanctuary.

Slithe sneered.
"Did your Father-Spirit warn you even against
        clothes?
Did He tell you clothes are only covered nakedness?
It's so like Him to fail to mention
That clothes designate all classes,
Otherwise we gods would look like mortals
And souls of honor and dishonor would look alike.
Clothes hide every blemish on the soul
And mask the body in whatever pretense we desire.
Clothes give life wonder
Then give us to the world
As we would like the world to have us.
Tell me *your* nakedness is innocence.
Tell me you have not in heart already undressed
        myself,
Wondering, if gods and mortals look alike.
Your husband's eye need never wonder,
Nor spend a moment of intrigue on you.
Shamelessly you give the sun itself full cognizance."

His words made her feel ugly,
Created as a barren thing of shame.
Then suddenly she straightened!
Shouting at the leering god,
"Both I and love came full at once,
My Father made my world and me,
As both of us should be.
Stag and doe dress not,
Their innocence clothes them with that same
        dignity
That Regis and myself do wear.

"Be gone,
What need have I of clothes?
You were wrong to come . . . !"

"Wrong to come?" The World-Hater sneered.
"I'm here at your request.
Last night as you fell asleep
You longed for evil,
Even after you had worshiped.
How like humanity to worship truth
And cherish evil in the same moment.
Let's get things straight, I do not barge
Into any soul unwelcomed by the heart.
You voiced aloud your need to see me.
I granted you your desire, that's all.
You will surely long again
And I will come again,
For evil is seasonal within the human breast."

"If I can wish you here,
Then I can wish you elsewhere.
Begone!" She shouted once again, "Now!"

And Slithe was gone.

But where he stood,
She found the ground chilled—
The grass, crystalline with frost.
"The white is beautiful,"
She mused, intrigued. "It's strange,
Where hate *and* knowledge bend to touch the earth,
The heart may long for truth, but doubt its worth."

The greatest sin
Is calling love, hate.
The second greatest sin
Is calling servanthood, ambition.
The list need go no further.
There are no other sins of
    consequence.

IX

She felt the frost upon the grass
Where Slithe had stood
And was startled to see
A serpent lying in the frost,
His frozen coils sheathed in ice.
His Arctic being lured Regina powerfully.
She longed to touch the chilling specter
But recoiled from her longing.
Her intrigue seemed to beckon him
And he slithered close and large.
Trembling at his size she reached
To touch his frigid skin.
She lifted him, and he felt heavy
As the cold stones of Sanctuary.

"Kiss me," hissed the snake,
"And I will make you wise."

She grimaced at the thought
And yet she lifted up the serpent
Until his giant hooded head
Was opposite her face.
His hypnotic yellow eyes
Forbid her own to look away.
His neck fanned wide and cold.
His leathered face darted toward her own,
Until his gleaming fangs fell knife-like on her face.
In the flash of pain,
She dropped the hideous creature
And running terrified to Regis, clung to him.

Regis saw the double marks
Where tiny drops of venom hung with blood.
"Are these the marks of broken trust
Upon your face?" he asked.

She started to reply,
But the swimming world left her
As the golden venom stirred a warm sensation
And exhilarating dreams were born.
In her light mind she left her leaden body
And lifted upward,
Until she left the forest far below.
In her wild delirium she saw that
Slithe rose too, a serpent floating
Idly, oddly, in the air.

Regina touched the marks upon her face,
Thrilling at the ecstasy of flight
Above her lofty view of Sanctuary,
She flew and marveled at her power.

The flying Serpent, soaring at her side,
Shouted through the high, thin air,
"All this I'll give you, If
You will call love, hate."

Swimming through her fantasies
She wept in dreaming echoes.
"Oh, give me flight and sight."

"Come," cried the flying cobra-thing,
They settled earthward from their odyssey
And glided to a grassy knoll of waiting splendor.
There, a mound of diamonds
Beckoned her as gleaming need
Cold as the crystal ice
That she had seen upon the grass
Where the serpent's sting had
Made her drunk with dreams.
She reached to scoop a handful
Of the crystalline fascination,
And then . . . the gems were gone—evaporated
    into air.

"Ah . . . ah! Diamonds have their price,"
Slithe taunted.
"These, my queen, are only yours
If you will call love, hate."

Again she didn't answer him.
Her dream was suddenly alive
With glorious music.

"Riches are no prize,
Only he who gives them." The reptile scoffed.
She watched him change.
He elongated and thickened
Into a handsome man.
The venom coursing through her soul
Crowned rich her fantasies with a strong and
        powerful longing.
Slithe, now handsome, clothed with glory, called
        aloud.
"O come, Regina, run with me,
The heathered meadows beckon."
Inwardly she barely could resist.

He called temptingly again, "Give me all that
        you give
Your mere, mortal mate.
And you shall know true knowledge.
I'll endow you with such ecstasy
As will open wide the gates of understanding.
We both shall know . . . be free . . .
Oh, call love, hate, and live!"

"Be gone, deceiver!" She called out,
Struggling through the sluggish stupor
Of her fading dream.

She shook herself
And woke in Regis' arms.

And there, leaning against him,
She sobbed that she had trusted hate
And felt ashamed that she had passed so near to folly,
"Regis, my heart draws close to treachery.
I reach for all I hate
And hate myself for reaching.

"Why do I sometimes crave
The taste of all I must not eat?
My mind is damned by needs
I am ashamed to name.
I can drive Him from Sanctuary
Any time I wish,
And yet I keep him near, wishing . . . longing . . .
Reaching for apocalypse,
And dying . . . Oh, keep me from desire.
Teach me to rebuke all treachery with reason!"

Regis interrupted her,
"Worship, Regina, will heal
Your dread caprice,
And teach you life in responsibility.
Worship and let love
Put lust away."

"Then come at once," she urged,
"Back to the grotto altar and let us
Cry out 'love and Father'
Till lust shall lose its place
To adoration!
Oh, Father-Spirit, hold my unsure hand
And bid me trust what I can't understand!"

Hate is absolute zero:
The state where all moisture
    crystallizes
And every structure explodes with
    cold.
There, all romance is but a winter's
    tale.
And dreams grow porcelain with hate
Till love shatters, along with lovers
Who thought love's warmth
Could bid the ice repent
And save its frozen soul.

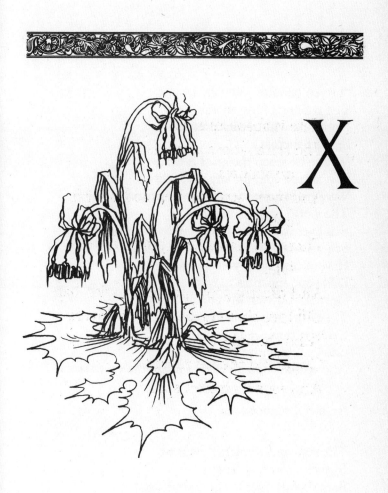

X

There's frost in Sanctuary!"
The Father-Spirit turned his head away in grief.
Regis and Regina were dumbfounded,
To know Earthmaker cried.

"You cry because of frost?"
Prince Regis asked.

"I weep because you willed
The coming of My enemy.
Notice how his recent presence
Spoils Sanctuary.
Where he stood the grass is dead—
The air too cold for any possibility of life.
Were he to have the scepter he desires
The world itself would die.
Evil lives in Sanctuary at your summons.
See his arctic scar on this good place.
Have you satisfied your longing?
Laid your appetites to rest?
Or, will you seek My enemy again
Till all this garden lies in ruin?
Can you now see how his hate
Can canker entire galaxies,
And spread contagions that infect the very stars."

An awful silence came.

The man and woman, downcast
In their shame, at length
Raised both their heads and pledged,
"Father,
Never shall we will
The death of love."

The Father-Spirit loved them.
"There is only one real power
That you should long to own: Self-denial!
Spend all you have to purchase it.
Lust after chains of servanthood—never thrones
     of pride.
For servants, worn by willful drudgery,
At last wear diadems.
Bridle all desire: For having what you want,
Will leave you groveling in wantonness.
Feed yourselves with hunger,
Then savor all you slowly eat.
Thus, self-denial will give you richness but
   keep you from excess.
Use this world, do not consume it.
Never pursue pleasure, rather let it find you . . .
At the end of every day . . .
Where you made discipline your friend.
For pleasure never comes in what you hold,
But in what holds on to you—compelling you
     to care.
Should life call you to be a martyr,
Do not despair
For those who would die for great reasons,
Also find great reasons for their living.
Think not that gaudiness is beauty
But simple ornament
Which lives only to reflect the light around it.
Turn from all desire to have,
Lest what you seek to own,
At last owns you!
Make no hour heavy with doubled greed
Rather let a giving spirit make you rich with
     sleek humility
That runs through troubled times.
Grow rich by giving up your purse.
Lay by your mace and rule.

Release your grasp and in your open hand
You'll find the world.
Die and greet the life-force
Created by your willful death.
For self-denial does empower the soul,
And those who hold their need to rule at bay,
Are kings and queens with empires in their sway."

Why do we long to touch
What we most fear?
Who can deny the cobra, deadly
   grace?
The luring symmetry of fanged face,
Yet if, spellbound, we reach
Into the serpent's place
Our life dissolves in venom with no
   trace.

XI

I could wish," sighed Regis,
"That there was something
Not quite human, not quite God.
Something knowing love
Yet touching hate."

The serpent suddenly was there.
Regis and Regina watched entranced as
The creature raised its glorious head
Into the morning sun.
Soon the Reptile eyes
Grew warm with life,
He spoke wistfully—like a king—
All recently deposed.
"Slithe I am now, but once
My name was Night Star.
I was and am and shall be
Brother to the light and to the dark.
I love all truth.
For I know the heart of falsehood
Is but integrity grown reasonable.
Good and bad are never values locked in stone,
They are only ways of seeing.

"To obey or disobey, is but artifice.
And nothing ever shall be right or wrong
Within itself.
If He who made you
Wags His finger in your face
Telling you love the good and fear the evil,
Remind Him you live free
Of all moral rigidity.
There is right that's only nearly right
And wrong that's not so wrong
And a lie that saves is better than destructive truth.

"And where's the trespass in a kind transgression?
Make your conscience judge
And you can purge the world of sin
And all the gods and devils will perish
With their good and evil categories.
Your Father lied to you.
There is no sin, till you define it so.
Sin is but the name of misery
That gods prescribe to make poor mortals fear
And teach them guilt.
What He calls 'sin' you've only to reverse and
Call it good.
Rename His old taboos,
And save your self from His confining moralisms.
You are guiltless when you say so,
Sin cannot live one second after *you* proclaim
        it dead!
Stroke my skin
And feel the innocence
We three shall share.
Let's take ourselves to bed."

"No! He warned us that intimacy can never be
        for three,"
Regis grew firm in his refusal.

"It is wrong? Sin, even?" Slithe scoffed.

"It is!" The Prince of Sanctuary
Now stood straight in his resolve.

"Wrong . . . Why? Is your nest too small?
Always wrong . . . evermore . . .
        eternity-without-end wrong?
Sometimes three can make the conversation ready,
The laughter frequent.
Think, man, and transform wrong to right.

Three is two grown generous.
My presence in the bower says that you both know
    hospitality
And kindness!
Since when is it a wicked deed to make space for
    a friend?"

And so that night the trio slept
Between the trees,
And when the morning came
Two humans and a snake
Woke in a common nest.
"Now see," Slithe said,
"We have done nothing wrong!
We spent the night as three
And yet we call it chastity!
Love's bed is big enough for all
Made broad by gracious minds."
He, slithering away, was swallowed up in dewy grass.
But the man and woman suddenly
Recalled Earthmaker's wondrous gift
Lamenting,
"Love for three can know no intimacy,
It spends it purse on grand obscenity."

Beware of mirrors
They lead us not to see ourselves
   But love ourselves
   Like poor Narcissus,
Who, grasping at his image died.
They say that floating in the
Water just above his
Wide-eyed, silent face
There was a butterfly.
Had he let it lead him into wonder,
He might have loved science, not
     himself,
And lived to cure the world of plague.

XII

The morning found Earthmaker
And His children
At the base of the two trees.

"Behold, the morning tree," the Father-Spirit said.
"At this tree's base is spade and hoe.
These tools invite you to deny mere ease
So the work to which you give yourselves
Can make your understanding grow."

Regis grabbed the spade
And turned the earth
Until his untried hands, wood-wounded,
Bled and blisters stung his fingers.
When he had stopped to rest
Regina spied two objects underneath the sunset tree.

She ran to them and Regis followed.
A crown and mirror leaning up against the bark
Allured her.

Regis and Earthmaker watched Regina
Place the crown upon her head,
And gaze into the mirror.
She was indeed a queen,
A Maya over paradise—
Beautiful and regal.

"Be not deceived, Regina," Earthmaker cried.
"Mirrors chain us to our vanity.
Serve and be free.
Leave off empty admiration and come to self-denial.
Cling to these tools!
Servanthood is better than acclaim.
The shovel breaks the hand in time,
But it is richer than this false crown.

Learn to spend yourself in work,
For though it cut the hands,
It dares to dream of changing
Desert into Paradise.
Work wears honor and
Shames all fruitless indolence.
Calloused hands made crowns look tinsel.
Work is pride.

"Work is glory.
Work is sweat in harvest fields—
The royal right to ask for bread.
Work teaches sleep to slumber, undisturbed,
And scorns to beg or steal.
Work alone understands the Sabbath truth
That six days of labor wakes the seventh day
     with honor.
And they who earn an honest Sabbath
Can worship Me, cleansing their fatigue."

Earthmaker walked to the mirror
And swung the golden circlet
Through the gleaming glass,
Shattering the image of a naked empress.
When the crown had melted into nothingness
The Father reached out to her.
"Your enemy has placed these objects here
To lure you into self-importance.
My little one, bridle your vanity—
Make self-denial the scepter of humility."
Earthmaker handed him the spade and her the hoe.
"Mirrors sometimes lead to false esteem
But spade and worship wash the desert green."

Unbridled lust:
A cannibal committing suicide
By nibbling on himself.

XIII

Regina woke before her mate
And saw the serpent rising
From the waters of the pool.

"Before your man awakes," the reptile hissed,
"Come with me, and I shall teach you choosing."

"Would I, who prize my husband's love,
Make any choice beyond his free consent?"

"Come not to choose,
But to consider choice.
Make yourself wise, then choose."
As she shrank away, he grinned,
"Do you recoil because you fear me?
Is my form strange to you?
Consider how much alike we really are."

He changed himself once more into a man,
Whose charm invited ease
And so she rose,
And looking down upon the sleeping form
Of her beloved, doubted.
She turned to Slithe.
Her doubts ebbed.
Suddenly she wanted something more . . .
A cleansing from the boredom of the hoe and
        spade.

"Should I worship?" she asked, half aloud.
"Yes," said the handsome tempter,
"But not Him who comes as wind!
Worship this," he said,
Gesturing to his powerful frame.
"And this," he said pointing to her body.

"Let us worship *us*, and knowledge will be ours.
Did you find the mirror and the crown I left at
          sunset?"

"I did, but they are gone now!"

"Gone . . . why gone?"

"My Father told me that to admire myself was most
          ignoble."

"Why? Did He not create you perfectly?
Surely beauty has some right to celebrate itself.
Before He woke you from the birthing altar,
He gazed as spirit-artist on what He had created,
Knowing you were the fitting finale
Of all that He had made.
Now He denies you mirrors?
When He admires you, it is mere artistry,
And yet when you admire yourself
It is evil vanity?"
He motioned unto her,
"Follow me."

She did.
They walked till they had
Left the bower far behind.
He took her hand.
His flesh felt cold.
She drew away.
And yet he would not let
Her hand escape his grasp.
"You are a goddess, beautiful.
Shout it without shame.
Vanity does not exist.
Like sin, it's missing from the healthy mind.
Your beauty calls to me,

And summons me to celebrate
What you must learn to celebrate: yourself!
I love you.
I worship you!
We shall do what we will.
The world is free of sin
For we decree it so!
Vanity begone!
Your beauty is an icon for us both."

They stopped. He faced her
Then he drew her close,
And holding her in an embrace
He whispered love
As bargains of betrayal.
"Fruit have I," he said,
"Whose life-red sap
Will teach your blood to sing."
His face moved toward her own
Till it filled all her vision,
And then he whispered,
"Regina, let your freedom flow as choice,
Kiss this bearded face, and hate will be for you
A glory warm as dust.
Feed hunger and embrace this craving night.
Let love grow generous with appetite."

A solitary soldier believed himself a
    regiment
And so he died, as he saw it,
A whole army felled with a single ball.
Fools are made secure by egotism
But the wise, knowing all their
    weaknesses,
Gather into troops
To walk through Dante's mind.

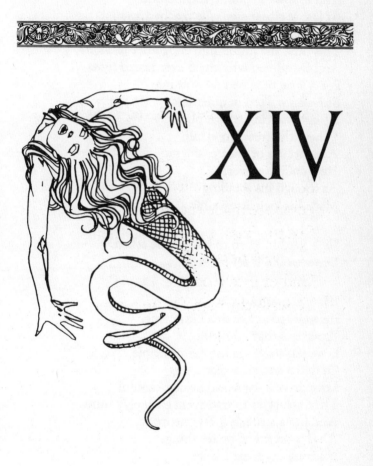

XIV

She tore herself away
Yet did not run . . . Slithe beckoned
And walked on.
Gradually she turned
And followed comfortably behind
At last at closer step, she reached again
To take his hand.
This time she found him altogether pleasant
And wondered why she'd ever feared him.
For a long time he said nothing.
She also walked in quietness.
At last, arriving at that place
Where the trees stood tall,
As sentinels of choice, she sat.
He stood, however,
As though his standing
Made his logic irresistible.

"Is it hard to learn to hate?" She asked.
"How would it set me free?"

"Hate comes easily,"
He smirked at her small knowing.
"Love it is that's difficult.
Love sets itself against the principle,
Of death and all defeat.
Love promises a world made beautiful
Then struggles to transform each ugly thing.
And in its struggle grows neurotic,
Always dreaming better things
Insisting upon excellence.
And excellence—demands, demands!
Never satisfied, and drives us
To compete with yesterday
And leaves us weeping that today
Is ever so much less than we had planned."

"Fair woman, I admire you
For abandoning your husband to look for love
Outside of your tight, cozy nest of mutual
    enslavement.
See how free you have become, away from Regis.
But you are still too much the slave of
Earthmaker's narrow requirements."

"Why should I hate? Why?
What in that bitter passion is divine?"

"Taste and see!
Come to knowledge and be free
Leave your humanness!
Be what you are: a goddess!
Close your eyes, Regina,
And see the glory that can be,
When you have the courage
To reach out for it."

She closed her eyes and in the darkness
Created by the simple act,
Slithe made her see a wondrous self.
She fell upon the warm red earth.
She lengthened in exhilaration
Till she was cobra-formed like Slithe.
They crawled as fast as eagles flew
And laughed in lusty sunlight.
They wound around the tree of choice
And climbed with coils of power
Till finally, high as serpents vie,
As cobras lying on the sky,
They reached the sun-red fruit.
"Give me, give me!" cried Regina,
Reaching fangward in the blue.

Regina's coiled form gave suddenly away.
She fell

And in her falling wept,
And hit the crusted earth
Then her awareness faded and was gone.

When her soaring reveries were dead,
She was alone and gasped to see
She held the blood-red fruit of choice.
Its shiny rind was still unbroken.
She knew she had not eaten.
She cast the fruit as far she might throw it
And hurried off to find the Prince of Sanctuary.
Behind her, low in gloating dust
The slit-eyed Slithe
Slithered on the pathway after her.
So evil always slithers after good
Drawing us with lust from "is" to "should."

Hate is born
When men call evil good.
And like an infant serpent
Bursting from its
Small, confining shell,
It never can be
Cased so small again.

XV

Earthmaker came at first light
Speaking directly to Regina.
"You've been with him?"

"I have,
For he draws me with such power
I feel that I must follow."

"Is he instructing you in hate?"
The Father-Spirit asked.

"He tries, but I'm committed unto love."

"Make sure your pledge,
Lest you in but a single taste
Devour your destiny.
Beware of compromise.
You play these days
Along the precipice
Of utter loss.
You've toyed so often now
with desperate caprice.
Indeed you've gone so far
You have only now to look on truth
And name it falsehood."

"I never shall!" the woman said.
But her speech fell slow
As if her promise lacked assurance,
Even to herself.
The forest sun fell in a compelling mood
Which leaked dividing shafts of light
Through all the leafy ceiling.
One of those rich rays
Fell upon the coils of
The fanged deceiver.

The snake lifting up his head,
Shouted at Earthmaker.
"Set her free!
Are You afraid
That given choice
She might choose wide enough
To be gods like You and me?
Regina, let not His Fatherhood
Call your bondage 'Daughter'!
Renounce Him!
He was my master only once.
Now I am free
Because of courage.
Your Father is afraid
That you, like me, will leave Him
And He will find Himself
Once more alone within the universe
He says He owns.
He sees—Don't you, Earthmaker?—
That you and Regis daily grow more hungry,
For all that He calls treachery
And I call utter liberty.
He hears already
How, the distant music comes."

"What music?" asked the woman.

"The music of denial.
The music of betrayal
Which will fill his private symphony
With raucous discord—
And bring at last true
Music to your life."
The serpent laughed
And slithered deep in shadows.

The woman turned imploringly,
"Father,

Must we ever live with him?
Take him from our sanctuary!"

"I did not bring him here.
I will not take him hence.
He came here at your will.
He will go of his accord
When you desire him gone.
Quit titillating all your appetites,
And Sanctuary will be free of him."

"But we have never asked him in this place,"
Regis spoke denial.

"Not in words, perhaps.
But what you harbor in your hearts,
Your tongues would scorn to speak aloud."

"Has the World-Hater always found
His joy in hate?" She asked.

"Hardly!" The Father-Spirit said.
"He was made to serve in love
But within him began to grow
The desire to have My place
And rule the stars on thrones
More lofty than My own.
He soon despised My realm and me.
Once he had cursed My love, he laughed at every
        dignity.
He plans the same cruel violence for you."

"Father," cried the man,
"Were we to choose the path of hate . . .
Would You still love us?"

"I would. I can do no other,
For love's the substance of My being.

But should you choose to call hate, love,
Ice like that which kills the grass
Around the World-Hater's feet
Would crush the glory of this glen
In icy tonnage, mauling Sanctuary.

"Consider the beauty of this realm and bid
Your appetites remember consequence.
Garrison your hearts.
Say no to all destructive lust:
Obey it and the blood of unbegotten empires
Will swallow Terra up in pointlessness,
A darksome world in search of self.
Which flies through night without identity
And wonders why she ever came to be."

The moth that trusts the candle's fire
Is willing martyr to her own desire.

XVI

With new resolve
The man and woman steeled themselves
Against all contemplation of disobedience.
They did not swear that they would never hate.
They, rather, lived rehearsing love.

So full was love's rehearsal
That when dawn awoke the pair
The Serpent was not there.
They found this no surprise,
For their thoughts were lost in adoration.

"Regina, morning wakes my heart," Regis spoke low,
"Daily now I try to measure
What I cannot measure, love! I love you,
With a love which leaps its high-walled doubts,
And lives to touch your face
And look into your eyes
Born like diamonds in the starlight.
Kiss me, and let your kiss be the pledge
That I will always hold you here,
Not just enriching Sanctuary
But making my life possible.
For without your love, I die—
As song, strangled into silence,
Or reason smothered by loneliness."

The morning found them wandering—
Walking, stopping to embrace,
Kissing first in shadows and then in sunlight.
For reasons only lovers understand,
She wove a chain of Hyacinth
And draped the lei
Across his chest and kissed him.
Then like a forest vixen

She exploded to a run
Teasing him with chase.
He pursued!
He caught her in the glade.
They fell laughing in the russet meadow.

"No life but this—forever," he shouted to the sky.
And they laid together,
Quiet in the splendor of soft breezes
And the warming of the sun.
"Today," he said, "Let's go to see the gates.
And celebrate ourselves
As we behold the barrenness
Of life beyond His care.
Perhaps in seeing this great emptiness
We'll find all sense rebuked
And know insanity for what it is:
Choosing any opposite of love."

They walked in silence through the day
Until at last they saw ahead of them
The gates of Sanctuary.
In hesitance at last,
They climbed the minarets
Which held the hinges
Of the lofty portals.

Far below them stretched the desert.
Where death rose up in dunes,
That seemed the burial mounds
Of civilizations still unborn.
Behind them Sanctuary rose
In lapis waterfalls, lavishly froth-dancing in cascades.

"Pray we shall never have
To live out there," the woman said,
Pointing sand-ward.

"Oh, Father," Regis prayed.
"May all You are, suffice us."

"Hold me," she pled suddenly startled.
He did but felt her trembling with old fears.
Something evil had
Brushed past her feet.

"Whatever is it?" he cried.

"Look," she pointed to the serpent
Now slithering to the highest ramparts
Of the northern spire.
There its circled shape
Left off its reptile form,
Rose, wavered, and
Untwisted into a man.

"Why is he here?" Regis asked her.
"Could you have desired his coming
In the face of this dead, desolate
Expanse of wasteland?"

"No," she cried.
"I never did desire his coming . . . I . . ."
Silence.
"Yes," she admitted at last.
"I . . . I only wondered
What it must be like
To walk in sand
When we have walked so long in paradise.
I only wondered if the desert . . ."

Her speech was interrupted
By the laughter
Of the World-Hater.

He stopped his mockery, shouting,
"This . . . not this . . . shall be your home."
His arm swept from the forest to the desert.
"You shall break these gates with courage
And live without these walls."

Considering his prophecy
And the desert out before them,
Regis shouted to his face:
"Go, Slithe, we are committed unto trust
We shall worship, with all loyalty,
Him who woke us unto life.
At the edge of emptiness we raise His name,
And celebrate the clay from which we came!"

Ego plays at life
To fill the hours with smiling politics
But only power can satisfy the
　　arrogant.

XVII

As they turned their backs
Upon the desert and started to descend,
Regina asked Regis,
"If the Father-Spirit rules the universe
Where is our dominion?"

"What need have we to rule?"

"I only wondered if all this land outside
Could be ours.
Could we own it, as he owns us?"

"What's there to own . . . but wasteland,
Shifting sands and howling winds?"

"Still, wouldn't it be better
To own a kingdom dry and dead
And have some throne, at least?
If we owned it as he owns this,
We'd both be Kings."

In the moment of her final sentence
Slithe reappeared smiling.
"There's a world out there
And room enough for all to rule.
You need but speak the word!
Then you will be like Earthmaker,
With power and scepter."

"But, Slithe, did you not once believe
That you could rule
In His expanded universe?
See what a wreck your own betrayal
Made of such assumptions."
Regis gestured toward the arid realm.

"But see," the World-Hater said,
"I can enter the world beyond these gates
As freely as I have entered Sanctuary.
You cannot.
You choose not to be king out there
And here you never can be king.
For here within these gates
He alone holds power.
The sand is empire waiting to be claimed.
Come rule! Know, and be gods."

"Leave us, Prince of Evil," cried Regis,
"You took the Diadem of Holy Love
Defiling it with pride.
Can you now claim to teach us virtue,
While your vile hypocrisy still hungers
To spread the wasteland of your banishment
Inside these walls of grace?
I have found you out,
PRETENDER! FRAUD! AND LIAR!
Life knows no more debauching infamy,
Than that which answers love with treachery."

"If you are the Son of God make this
    stone bread."
"I will indeed," the false messiah said.
"And from this stone nearby, I shall
    make wine."
Thus greed can fill a glutton's plate
And utter selfishness may dine.

XVIII

Will the Father-Spirit
Really drive us from this place?
If He has so much power
Could He not pinch some little corner
From His Kingdom and offer it to us?"

"Please Regina . . . careful . . . lest you call
        love hate.
Let's go once more
To the grotto altar and bow in adoration.
Let us whisper 'Love' and 'Father'
And adore the Spirit that enfranchised
Our once-dead clay with Life."

"No . . . husband . . . go alone.
I've lost my taste for worship now.
I need to be alone to think."
She walked away in ponderous melancholy.

Regis also walked alone in heaviness.
He wondered just how often in these latter days,
His woman talked with Slithe.

He passed a lionness and lion
And remembered how alone he once had felt.
Love was somehow dying,
And even as he clung to it
It sifted, sand-like, through his longing fingers.
He recalled old joys—
New love, touching as first splendor.
His mind was camera to hurried scenes
Of laughing lovers running in the sun.
A sudden, scalding grief made his body shudder.

He wandered, as though the night
Refused him anything

But grieving darkness.
At length his aimless feet came across an old path
That he and his now doubtful queen
Had often walked together.
A chilling fear seized him
As he saw the naked footprints
Of his beloved
Wandering in soft earth.
For there the small depressions
Of her feet
Mingled with the curious, soft,
Embossing serpent trails.
He pondered those strange trails
And asked himself how long
Could Sanctuary live.
These days were hurtling to ruin
As though their eager pace—
Made furious by every dread he felt—
Could barely wait to stab at Fatherhood.
Life in the bosom of great love, was ebbing.
Life as he had known it, dreamed it, clung to it
Was dying.

His tears fell in the dust,
Making visible coagulations of his grief
Among the slithering indentations,
Of a serpent's belly
And the footprints of his own beloved,
        thoughtless queen.
He cried aloud, stretching his entreaty
Toward the heavens—
Grasping nothing in his closing fingers:
"Choose wisely, Queen, remembering the cost
Lest love and sanctuary both be lost!"

A beggar asked a millionaire,
"How many more dollars
Would it take to
Make you truly happy?"
The millionaire,
Reaching his gnarled hands
Into the beggar's cup, replied,
"Only one more!"

XIX

When the sun was high
Regis found Regina piling fruit
From the morning tree.
She stacked it feverishly
With nervous hands
That flew about their task.
Her eyes were crazed
By some wild drivenness.
When the stack seemed
About to tumble,
Regis, reached out asking, "Why?"

"So there will be enough for tomorrow."

"There has always been enough.
Abundance, here, is great as love.
It always comes with sunrise.
Have His blessings ever failed us?
Have we ever woke in Sanctuary
With too few evidences of His care?
See, already, what a waste
Your greed has made.
The fruit at the bottom of your pile
Begins to darken.
On the tree it would have been connected
To the source of life
And lived until we needed it.
What sudden spirit in you
Stores this rotting fruit
Against your insecurity?
Has the serpent led you even more
Into his web of doubt?"

"Regis! I will not have you slur the Serpent!
He is friend, mentor, healer unto me.
He makes me doubt only that

Which should be doubted.
He said that life
Can interrupt itself with pain.
See this scar?"
She held her wrist to him.
"I got it picking berries
When a tiny limb
Thrust its knife-like branch
Into my hand.
But when the serpent came
I felt much better."

"Then why this dying pile of fruit?"

"Because Slithe says that life is fragile . . .
Think, Regis! Open up your eyes!
The Serpent's words may save us!
If we should have to live
Beyond the gates
We could carry all this fruit
Into the fruitless desert
And there we still might live."

"Regina!" Regis was surprised
To find himself so near to shouting.
"There is no life beyond the gates!
There is no love beyond the gates!
There is no walk with
Our beloved Father there!"

"Slithe says the sand is warm in sunshine.
He claims there is no foliage there
To block the stars at night.
And that the desert sun rises clear
Unobstructed by the forest.
He counsels us that it is better to be free
In glorious sand than to be chained
In Paradise by love.

He says there is a certain thrill
In disobedience that we have never known . . .
That ecstasy more often comes,
Not in what is right
But in what is nearly right—
And great exhilaration comes
In what is clearly wrong.
O, Regis, why can we not trust him . . .
At least a little?
We trust the Father-Spirit.
The Hater says that we have grown—
Too stingy in our trust.
That life is broader
Than the narrow cell that
We have built ourselves
From his confining love."
She paused a moment . . .
"Oh, I am learning much from Slithe!"

The man stood silent.
He looked again
At the dying pile of fruit and said to her,
"When will you have enough
In this decaying pile
To make you feel content?"

"I just need a little more."
She turned and picked another piece
And laid it on the pile.
She walked away, hurried,
As though she had
Some frenzied business to attend.
He watched her till she passed
A sunlit section of the path
And then he saw her pick up something
And hold it to the sky.
She was holding up the serpent,
Swirling him in golden ecstasy.

Tears flooded Regis' sight,
Washing his despair into a blur,
Till in the distant circle of the sun,
The snake changed to a man,
Who then lifted Sanctuary's queen
And held her up, exulting.
Their playful laughter,
Stabbed Regis
With a killing numbness.
He stumbled to his knees
Burying his torn face in his hands
While they hurried on into the depth of green
And their laughter died away.

Regis wept!
The fruit that now lay dying on the ground
Was too obscene to hold his interest.
Disconsolate, he made his way
To that warm place
They once had called their nest.
There the sun came slow and late,
And the sapphire pool
Colored early afternoons.
He sat, in thought,
Reflecting by the water
For quite some time
Before he noticed
An odd collection of leaves
Knit together in a strange fashion.
When he picked the leafy object up
It appeared a crude kind of garment . . .
Like the one the Hater wore, only shabby.
He knew his woman had fashioned it,
So that she could be like . . .
He stopped his mind,
"Come, O Father-Spirit, and draw near.
Rebuke these doubts which circle me with fear."

The illicit
Does not exhilarate.
It but indicts:
The sweetness of all adultery
Leaves just before the splendor,
Destroying the ecstasy
We thought might linger
To eliminate the shame.

XX

This is the place of choice!"
Slithe encircled her and asked,
"Are you afraid?"

"And what is fear?" She laughed.
"The choice of timid men
Who live in bondage.
Have I told you of the joy
I feel with you?
So long I have obeyed
The strict confinement
Of the Father-Spirit's world.
Now I shall declare
That I am free . . .
Free and I will choose at last,
Even as a goddess.
I shall live in Sanctuary
Or wherever I shall choose.
But I shall choose."

Slithe slipped into his other form.
His handsome body dwindled, shrinking
Until his serpentine remains
Curled at her feet on the brilliant turquoise
Floor of Sanctuary.
He then twisted around her legs
And rose in circling coils
About her naked body.
At last she took him from her upper bosom
And gazed into his slitted eyes.
His mouth broke open
And his fangs dropped gleaming white
Into the sun.

"You can't frighten me," she laughed once more.
"Today is my day to be free of fear.

Today . . . I choose . . . I make my own way."
She set the serpent on the ground
And felt exhilarated—like a queen—
Queen Regina, sceptered by her daring.
She ruled and watched her serpent king,
And smiled in giddiness,
Naïveté crowned by adolescent vanity.

As his simple queen looked on,
Slithe slithered to the tree of choice,
The tree of freedom . . .
The tree of knowledge . . .
The tree of living where she would.
The tree that promised
All the warmth of desert sand
And sunrise brilliantly inflamed.

She watched, mesmerized
As Slithe picked fruit
By nipping stems
With gleaming teeth.
One piece fell,
And it settled ever downward
In a floating fashion.
But before it hit the ground
Slithe, himself, was somehow there.
He caught it as it dawdled earthward
And extended her the fruit.

"Eat and take it to the man!"

"He will not eat!"

"He will!" The World-Hater cried,
"For what I could not achieve with him
You will.
For he will not permit in you
What he does not find within himself.

You see, I am content to be alone.
And so for that matter is your Father-Spirit.
But you and the man need company.
It will be no time at all before
He feels again the same, old killing loneliness
That once made life unbearable.
He will eat, dear Regina, he will eat."

"But let us not spoil this moment."
He led her to a shaded portion
Of the grove.
They leaned back against a tree.
He embraced her as she lifted
Life's denial to her lips.
She ate, and in the glory of the taste
Her world shook beneath her.
The stars spun above.
Vision blurred
And the green of Sanctuary shouted
Hues of wild and waxen glory.
Her whole body seemed alive, afire,
Shot through with
Passing currents of night storms
Electrified with forked glory.

But in a moment the ecstasy was gone.
She stood alone . . . And naked . . .
Odd, now she knew both words at once
And yet to be both "alone" and "naked"
Were heavy terms of judgment.
When shame arrives
We somehow must have company.
And so the naked queen clutched both fruit and
        shame
And hurried off
To seek a reinstatement
Of lost innocence.
Her face—no, all her being—

Was flushed with hot despair.
Tears tracked like crackling porcelain
Yet cut like molten stone into her faithless
     stammering.
"My treachery lies as burning disobedience.
My foolish ecstasy was but
The ash of momentary fire.
Oh, Regis, please forgive my wretched sin.
Your love alone can make me clean again!"

The wings of demons are as white as
    angels' wings
Their halos are as golden bright
They sing as well as angels, too
But only when it's night.

XXI

Regis came upon Regina holding
To the half-eaten fruit.
She was singing softly to herself,
Unaware that in the leafy walls
Of a now alien forest
Her beloved heard her song.
Here and there her broken soul
Ruptured her lament and choked the music of
Her requiem for love.

"A flash of pleasure have I bought with pain—
A tiny moment's hurried ecstasy.
And I have sullied love with stain
And answered faith with treachery.
Once both our world and love were shining new.
Then we took pleasure in the golden leas
And laughed as lovers laugh—·all noble, true—
And felt the thrill of honest ecstasy.
But here I hold the witness in my hand,
The sticky sweet of all my appetite.
My craven lust to call rank evil, grand—
The queen of sun, gone whoring after night.
I wore the crown of Terra, and I owned
The portion of a queen. I loved a king
Whose gentle arms forbade me walk alone.
Whose husky voice made Sanctuary sing.
Our palace was of beams left whole inside
The trees. And stones unquarried were the tower.
The wife of Regis soon became the bride
Of greed, the mistress of the dog of power.
O Regis, kiss our love in requiem,
Lament the queen who laid her scepter by.
Who cast off sense, called pleasure whim,
And taught the sanctuary sun to cry.
Forgive your soiled queen her soiled crown.
Who saw love everywhere, yet reached for lust.

Who pulled her sky-born king to naked ground
And chained her sky-barred eagle in the dust."

The music ended,
Regina turned toward the trees
Where Regis waited
And in an instant
Each saw the other.

"Regis . . . Regis . . . King!" the woman cried,
She ran to him,
"Hold me, so I will
No longer be alone."

"But you've never been alone!"
He said as he embraced her.
"You're trembling," he said.
He was devastated to find her
Innocence so scarred,
To see her
So encased in moods of fear
That he had never known.

"I'm so afraid!" she blurted
Clinging closer than she ever had.

"Alone, afraid?
I heard your Requiem . . .
You've tasted the forbidden?"

"Oh . . . I have eaten . . . Eaten!
I have known such ecstasy
As you cannot imagine.
I felt the glory of this place . . .
Of nakedness . . . and . . ."

"And only now do you know nakedness . . .
Have your deeds

Undressed your heart?
Do you love me, Regina?"

"Yes, yes! I love all but him.
Him I hate . . . Slithe!
The World-Hater!
Do you not hate him too?'

"I do not hate at all . . .
Nor am I lonely or afraid . . ."

"Eat with me," she begged,
Pulling the piece of fruit
From behind her back.
"Leave me not alone.
Don't you see our world is now divided
Into fourths?
There is the hater,
Your Father-Spirit . . ."

"He used to be *your* Father-Spirit too,"
He cried in interruption.

"Fourths . . ."
She put his speech aside . . .
"Yes . . . Fourths . . . Your Father-Spirit,
The Hater . . . my lonely self and you.
For you, too, are alone.
You are as alone in your faithfulness
As I am in my deceit.
I cannot stand this wall between us."

"Deliver me . . . please love me
More than Him who gave us Sanctuary
And then each other.
I know He'll come
And drive me from this place.
I cannot face the desert by myself.

Please, eat!"
He watched her piteous pleading
As his mind recalled her little pile
Of dying fruit and realized
The Hater had bade her trust a lie.

Regis turned from her and walked away.
His heart was crushed by her entreaty
And the love he held for Earthmaker.
He knew he could not please them both.
His agony no longer sought
To make a choice of living free or captive.
His was the necessity of choosing
When every choice was wrong.

If he ate not
She'd die alone in bleakness.
And if he ate he'd crush the heart of his Creator.
He paused beside the sapphire pool, looking down.
He studied his tired face.
It cracked in pain and fell away.
"My wife, my Father: Which shall I choose?
Oh, Father,
If I should try to tell the fullness of all meaning,
The very reason I find existence dear,
The inwardness that makes me eager to awake,
They all should spell one word, 'FATHER!'
I swell when I behold Your coming in the rain,
I thrill to feel Your sunlight on my skin.
You are all in all to me.
I have been loved by love too powerful
To occupy any mortal form
Or try to case itself in anything,
That may be touched.
You meet me in my worship . . .
Caress me as wind . . . end all my loneliness,
And best of all You call me 'SON!'
Never has Your love awakened me,

But that I adore the light,
And speak love's holiest name, 'FATHER!'"

"But, O my beloved!"
He saw Regina in his mind and spoke to her,
"If, besides His love that gave me being,
I should be given just three syllables,
And then commanded never more to speak,
Those glorious syllables would be 'REGINA!'
And they would be enough to say
That when a man is touched
By love's full presence,
His life was worth the clay.

"Regina, you were my morning,
And the sun looking down on our relationship
Cursed his distance from this planet.
The stars at night
Saw themselves reflected in your eyes
And damned their lack of brilliance.
And when I kissed you in the fields,
I knew that life would give me ecstasy,
But for the asking.
And when the ecstasy arrived,
I measured splendor by the sky-fulls.
O Goddess, did I worship you too much?
Did I cherish you beyond the strength
I needed just to hold
To what my soul adored?
Now at last, this double love
That made me rich, steals everything.
And leaves me groveling in loveless poverty,
Where ardor lies, at last, in ashes.
Regina . . . queen! Earthmaker . . . Father!
O agony that is mine, to love both you and Him.
I cannot force my undeciding heart
To spurn my wife and take my Father's part."

"Bring me a long, warm coat."
"You must be freezing."
"No, just ashamed."

XXII

Regis wandered through the days.
From time to time he studied
Those huge trees that marked the place of choice.
He doted on Earthmaker's love,
And their delight before the woman came . . .
Before the serpent ever coiled in pristine sunlight
Infecting simple beauty with disease.

He thought about his great delight
When first the woman blessed his world.
He called to mind their walks,
The closeness of her warmth . . .
The sweet smell of her hair
When his chest
Was pillow to her head.
He thought of paradise . . .
Of Sanctuary and wished it wider.
And then in chilling inwardness
He thought of all the endless miles
Of stretching desert that lay beyond the walls,
And those high gates that sealed them in.
He shuddered to think that those same gates
Would shut out his beloved
And seal him in, alone, forever!

And then, could he expect the Father-Spirit
To fashion him a new, unspoiled love?
Could he start again with some new Regina
Made to end his aching loneliness once more?
But he wanted no "new" Regina—
Only she who first reigned over terra with himself.

Suddenly he froze.
He had not seen Regina
During the sojourn of his brokenness.
Might the Father-Spirit already have set her
Beyond the gates?
The question drove him in haste

To seek the bower again.
It was there that they had recently separated.
He called to her. She did not answer.
Certain now that
She must already be outside of Sanctuary,
He called to her again.
He ran in frenzied need but could not find her.
Weary with the agony of searching,
He fell asleep
And waited for the coming of the Father-Spirit.
He dreamed of his beloved wandering the desert,
Lamenting her treachery.

When he awoke he was gloriously aware
Of Regina's wondrous form
Nestled there beside him.
He felt her body shivering
Even as he drew her close.
Her pain was his pain now.
"Earthmaker will soon come and separate us.
You can no longer live in Sanctuary."

Suddenly he knew what he must do.
"Give me the fruit.
I'll eat.
We'll leave together."

"No, please!" she begged;
She'd clearly changed her mind.
"At first I wanted that, but I see more clearly
You've done nothing wrong.
He will not punish you for my sake.
Stay here and live.
Do not commit my folly."

"To live alone
Is not to live at all!" he cried.
"I once lived alone—Nevermore!
Give me the fruit!"

"I don't know where it is!" she lied.
Lying was easier for her now.
She was glad it was permitted.
For it seemed one simple lie
Would save her beloved
Even as it condemned her to exile.
But it was to little avail.
For even as she lied, he saw the truth:
The fruit lay beckoning like sunset.
For her the fruit was sweet at first taste.
For him all that remained was galling emptiness.
He grabbed at disobedience, choked at the sourness!
The sap was liquid fire
That spun a dream of futile reaching.
His Father walked away from him
As he reached out
And grasped the empty air.
"Loss . . . loss . . . loss . . ."

His dreaming cried—
The trees of Sanctuary withered.
The gates were closing him outside.
His Father turned with reaching
But his own weak stretching arms
Were far too short.
Then came the dark.
He groped in blindness in the desert
Crying as a child in the night.
"Father, Father, Father,
Forgive! Forgive! Forgive!"

He woke to find,
The crying of his dream was real.

They both sobbed now ashamed
Of all they had done.
And clinging to each other
In the face of coming night,
They waited for the dawn's first beckoning
To call their faithlessness to reckoning.

They say that dying often brings
A hurried cinema of all our lives.
In its spastic flashing reels is Adam
Trying hard to hold to oily Eden,
Weeping as it slips away.

XXIII

They came at last—old enemies—
Whose warring hostilities had fallen
On the battlefield of two weak human wills.

"Will you walk them to the gates,
Earthmaker, or shall I?"
The World-Hater mocked.
"Look," he laughed at their crude coverings.

The man and woman looked down
At the hastily appointed leafy shields
They had draped about themselves
In a vain attempt to hide from the piercing eyes
    of Him
Who looked through skin and so beheld their
    hearts.
They only stood in silence—
Wishing themselves smaller.
Begging inwardly that the distant mountains fall
    upon them.

"It is the end of dignity," the Hater gloated.
"See them now, Earthmaker, made little by their
    infidelity.
Now they hate—so far only me . . .
But soon, perhaps, each other.
And, oh, the glorious hate of all of their
    descendants,
That, in millennia to come, shall battle-bleed Your
    world!"

The Father-Spirit grieved.

The Hater gloated, "I once served at Your right hand
And knew Your promises!

It was too small a gift then—it is too small now.
These two have found that Your esteem
Was not the altar they desired . . .
They wanted what I wanted . . .
And what you never seem to share . . . *power!*"

"Power," the Father-Spirit murmured,
Only slightly louder than the brook
That splashed in white through Sanctuary.
"Power is only grandeur to him who wields it.
To those who languish underneath its crushing
        heel,
It destroys every shred of dignity."

A silence followed and the Hater hissed,
"Behold Your fallen royalty."
He gestured to the couple
Who listened, wounded at their conversation.
"Their nakedness is inward—
And yet they feel it outward.
Their fallenness delights me.
Homo Sapiens,
Man the knowing! Indeed!
Hah!
Homo Horribilis!
Alas, if knowing only made him good!
But see your lovers wrapped in shame!
Their children's children will
Lay waste each other
In a hundred thousand, pointless wars—
Each one based on hate.
Today, Earthmaker,
I close the garden of Your hopes.
Go ahead! Try to sell each coming generation
        peace!
They'll always come to me for apples!"
He sneered, then laughed,

Till his laughter leapt to howling!
When howling finally folded to a hiss
He dwindled earthward and slithered off.

"Come," the Father-Spirit beckoned, "Come . . ."

The man looked at his wife and said,
"We must leave now."

The three walked together for the last time
On the shaded paths they once enjoyed in hope,
When new laughter
Was the raucous joy
Announcing man had come.
Now a pall of silence shrouded them with pain.

The Father-Spirit spoke at last,
"There is coming to the world you will inherit
A Singer who will sing a song of dignity and life.
And Terra, in a happier age shall see Sanctuary
        born again."

"Beyond these gates
Life will be hard.
And worse, it will be temporary.
But remember my promise: a Singer,
That you may live without despairing."

They reached the towers
Which rose like monuments of exile,
To mystify the tiny pair
Now dwarfed by their betrayal.
The woman wept!
The man comforted her.
Slowly they moved past the minarets.
The gates stood open only for a moment,

Silhouetting them against the sand.
And Regis, reaching up to heaven cried—

"Hell is a lust for dark by those in light.
Our infamy has conquered day with night!"

The gates clanged shut—

Every baby comes as evidence
That God still dreams of Eden.
Sift Messianic mangers, and you'll
    find
Wherever Spirit and the flesh connect,
Wherever time and Ages intersect,
Some loving God lies in a human nest
And suckles milk at a Madonna's
    breast.

XXIV

The days were long
And marked by murderous work
For both of them,
And yet they always longed
To see each other
In the first light of morning.

"I love you," said Regina, now grown older.
"And today when the stones cut your hands
And the ground
Resists your efforts to bring life,
Remember this—I love you."

He looked at her hair,
Already streaked with gray
And knew in time
Their eyes would no longer hold the light,
Nor view the mountains they had grown to love.

"The years steal life.
I shall not always be here
Nor shall these eyes forever gaze
Upon the face for which I traded immortality."

"There is something I must tell you," said the
        woman.
"It will make your time in the fields much shorter.
I am with child—
A child, who like ourselves, may make the wrong
        choices
But here and there he may choose right.
And we, as our Father-Spirit promised,
Will have a chance
To start again
With life in innocence."

He embraced her
It seemed a sign.

And so the planet Terra came to be.
It circled through wide fields of stars
And waited, and in the waiting
Lay the glory of a promise
Living side by side with pain.
In time the hurt would die
For a promise always outlives pain.

Time watched the exiled king and queen
Till in the autumn of their lives
They both were overcome by visions of such power
They shielded their weak eyes
Against the burning dream.

They saw beyond their sight the dark frontier,
Of a cosmos, cold and comatose.
A storm of brilliant comets
Flew on wings of fire.
Earthmaker shouted to shy galaxies,
"Be born and shatter night!"

In fiery happenstance
Were born a thousand suns,
And their light fell, light-years away
Upon a solitary Troubadour walking starward
Toward waiting Terra.
The planet trembled the very instant
That the Singer's feet left atmosphere
And fell upon the desert floor.

Regis and Regina reached out to Him as He
       passed by,
Walking toward those gates
Sealed shut by rusting years.

The Singer saw a serpent rising in His path
And placed His foot upon its ugly head
Till all the writhing stopped,
And the reptile burst to flames
Beneath His feet.

Still on He walked, promethean in power,
Unto the towering gates.
He raised his hands, doubled them to fists,
And struck the ancient barriers with force.
They splintered into ruin
And fell—iron, wood and stone—in rubble.
From the long sealed-sanctuary
Eager water gushed,
As though it were alive,
Into the desert.

The vision faded.
Regina saw that it was but a dream and wept.
Regis took her in his arms
And whispered to her lost illusions,
"One day, Regina . . . . One day,
This dream is but His truth
Come early unto us
From age to age
The hope shall live until He comes."

In dimensions His two children
Would never understand,
The Father Spirit drew the blue, green planet
To His bosom and shouted to the stars,
"One day, beloved world, one day!"

A
SYMPHONY
IN SAND

Once in every universe
Some world is worry-torn
And hungry for a global lullaby.
O rest, poor race, and hurtle on through
    space—
God has umbilicaled Himself to straw,
Laid by His thunderbolts and learned
    to cry.

I

A solitary Child sat playing in the sun.
He lifted sand by chubby handfuls
Dropping it in gold cascades
That made the desert laugh.
His young and powerful guardian
Stood by, devouring Him in steadfast gaze.
At length, the tall man knelt
And reached out to the Child.
The Boy extended him
A grip of desert sand.
His guardian then took the dab of gold,
And poured it gently on the Infant's head.
Even as the sand fell desert-ward
The man's smile broke as sunlight
Erupting in pronouncement,
"Earthmaker, Glorious, be baptized
With the very earth You formed."
The gold trickled through his fingers
In showers of dancing diamonds,
That splashed upon the Child.

Above the man and Child
High rusted, ivied gates stretched upward.
The ancient doors were
Hinged to mossy granite.
Old hate-begotten grudges
Still seemed to cling in gray and green
To desolate and crumbling stones.

The towering man beneath the somber
        gates
Traded his light and lilting liturgy
For a vaulting and vivacious shout
That gobbled up the silence of the place,
"Live, Boy, till these old gates
Be shattered and sanctuary opens wide

To hold the wedding rites of God and
    humankind.
Live, I say, till every earthly desert
Repents its barren sands,
And gives birth unto a river.
Then shall all men lay by their swords
To gather holy rust
And laughing mothers hold their children
Unafraid of plague.
Grow manward, Boy,
Till hate at last smelts daggers
Into spoons and feeds its enemies. . .
Till tyrants give their dungeon keys
To priests and the blood-rich soil
Of battlefields grows grain
To feed the soldiers
Of a finer cause.
Grow older, Child, and as You grow,
The putrid halls of death shall change to healing
    rooms
Where sickness may meet sunlight.
Clap little hands till, wounded,
Your strong fingers shall
Strangle all the pointless causes
That eat up human hope.
Dance little feet until your injured footprints
Shall explode with fire enough to
Sear the wounds of violence
And every planet sings a better song!"

His rhapsodizing stopped at once!
He drew his sword.
"Declare yourself!"
He roared into the thick green shadows
That gathered in the stubby wood
Behind the wide-eyed Boy.
"The Child has come!
It is the Age of the Convergence!"

The word "convergence" floated heavily
Threading its way into a serpent's den.
The reptile woke!
Two yellow eyes snapped open.
Coral gold and black unbraided all in liquid
    movement
As he slithered into sun.
He fanned his neck,
Rearing, half-length, until his shadow
Fell across the Boy.

The Child was unafraid.

"So the Convergence comes at last!"
The reptile hissed.

"It does."

"And you've come here to these old walls
To announce this final shining age. . . ."

"I have!"

"What irony,
That His eternal fanfare should sound first
Here at the very gates
Where I defeated Him!
When last these old doors swung
There passed a man and woman,
Who traded innocence for knowledge
And found that they were gods,
Albeit, most unhappy gods!"
If serpents may be said to smirk,
The haughty cobra grinned at the Child.
"So this is Earthmaker!
Tell me, is He vision or reality?
As He is or shall be?"

"Is or *was* or *shall be*
Are but the piteous
Categories of those who have
So little time they must divide
It into then or now.
This Child is God made man,
And, as He *is* He *shall be*.
Earthmaker shall enwomb Himself in innocence,
Umbilical Himself to need,
Crying out at cold damp midnights,
Whimpering in dependency for human milk."

"Then this small thing which I behold
Is great Earthmaker in rehearsal to be man?"

"He needs no practice, Slithe,"
The man stared firmly into the reptile's eyes,
Whose gaze broke under his authority.
"The heaviness of glory
Demands His gentle form come slowly.
For Terra is an old woman now.
And spinning slow of age,
She wobbles in her palsied orbit.
Should all His vastness come too suddenly
On this uncertain world
His splendor would destroy it."

The serpent hissed a grinning joy.
"I'm glad He comes a Child
For children are an easy mark for evil.
I shall play about His cradle
And envenom all His dreams
Till dragons stalk His sleep."

The Child laughed and scooped
The sand and held it outward
To the serpent.

Ansond joined the Child in glee
Until their double laughter climbed the ivied walls,
"See, Slithe, He's unafraid!
He's armored by a kind of power
Your fangs can never pierce!"

"No power is so unwoundable!"

The golden man reached up with doubled fists,
Enraged by crass audacity,
"How naive is evil!
Behold the power of Holiness!
This aging world can never stand
Before the sway of purity!
His is the power of innocence
That grows from new, chaste love,
And holy inwardness.
This Child, unspoiled by power,
Can fear no serpent, hear no threat,
Or know no terror in the night!
Coil all around His cradle, if you will.
He will but stroke your head
With gentle hands
And bless you with the force of love
Born in His own unfearing eyes.
Innocence can sleep among the wolves
        untroubled.
It distills like dew
In sweetest sunrise
And plays untroubled in the maw of hell.
Innocence is deaf to thunder,
And made so rich by lavish trust
It never thinks of poverty.
For butterflies are gold
And rainbows are the emerald crowns
Of kings who never have learned fear.
It's innocence that gives the gracious wind its
        strength

And lifts the fragile flowers into the gales
And smiles at sifting petals."

"Sheer poetry, Ansond."
The serpent sneered
Then thickened to a man.
They quarreled, but
The Child who was between them
Played unaware of all their rhetoric.
"Ansond, you forget so soon our ancient grudge.
It burns no slower now than it did then
In the war of realms—
Where sword to sword we fought."

"No, Slithe, I could never
Let that horror slip from mind.
The universe itself recalls your blasphemy!
How painful yet the memory!
I begged you then to return to Him who gave
You being—You would not and lost all!"

"Not lost—but gained all!
This planet now is mine—this entire realm!
You've nothing, Ansond . . . nothing!"

"Wrong! Krystar!" Ansond
Used the serpent's older name—
"These I have!"
He tore his tunic off!
His bronzed chest was laced with silver scars!
"These, lost friend, are the marks of loyalty!
I bear each one in honor, and yet
My scars do not compare
With those this Child will one day wear!"

The World Hater stepped toward the Boy
And reached to Him as if to pick Him up!
Instantly, the gold man stepped between them

And in that single step was transformed to a lion.
The Hater shrank in terror,
Dwindling downward to a snake again.
In but a moment the old foes
Faced each other as lion unto cobra,
Power confronting power with fierce defiance.

The lion roared and circled
The still untroubled Child.
He nudged the Child with his broad nose,
And both of them walked slowly off.
Their substance thinned as they moved outward
Toward the fruitless plain,
Losing firmness even as they walked.
Their opaque blurs of vanishing reality
Dimmed to a haze that fled the cobra's straining
        eyes.

"So this was only an illusion.
There is no Child . . . no lion. . . !"
The cobra hissed into the desert air.
The desert chose to take the part of truth
And shouted in reply!
"The Age of the Convergence dawns.
Let every mountain range declare with joy
The lion roars and God is born a Boy."

A heavy crown
Can force the face of any weary king
Toward the ground.
But here and there wise kings
Bid crowns good-bye—
And find without their crowns
They're light enough to fly.

II

It was night, the time
When Melek most felt his years.
His queen was dead—long dead.
A decade of cool desert nights
Had come and gone since
She had slept that final sleep
Where waking is forbidden.
For as many nights he'd sat alone
Upon the balustrade
Of a palace he must soon leave kingless.

Melek knew the stars.
They were his friends—his only friends.
They understood his longings!
He ached for things that could not be
And wished he could restore the past . . .
If only one of his lost sons had lived!
But alas he had no child, no heir, no hope—
No kingdom and no king to follow him.
He stood and leaned far out
Above the cracked-tile roof.
"Loneliness numbs thought," he mused.
"And older sight sees only things
That clearly say they're here.
Poor eyes do not betray me.
Be either blind or honest.
For what I now see on the garden lawn
Defies all sense and yet forbids
Me look away."

A vision stopped his words:
A single Child
Sat playing in the starlight.
The Boy lifted up his head
And smiled so broadly that it seemed
His smile would gather all the fading light,

Then wash old Melek's vision black.
The aged sovereign rubbed his eyes and laughed
    aloud.
"Dead palace . . . empty courts.
How long since your gray walls
Have seen a Child?
Earthmaker, play no tricks on me.
I've lived alone too long.
Call yourself no God of mercy
If this Child be not real!"

His weary legs at once grew young!
His feet flew as though his
Queen were yet alive
And there to bless his coming.
Down, down, down,
And nimbly—too—he clipped
The steps from balcony to garden.
When he had turned past hedge
And wall, he cried aloud . . .
"The Child *is* here and He is *real!*
But stop . . . and slowly now . . ."
He checked his furious pace,
Lest his starving longing
Frighten the Child into devouring shadows.
Old and young they stared—
Eye to eye—each moved faceward
Toward the other.

With trembling hands the old one reached out first
    to touch . . .
To let his fingers test his vision.
His joyous touch approved his sight!
He gave a little cry!
The Child too reached out
Begging with His eyes.
Melek slipped his hands beneath the Boy's arms
And lifted Him.

Crushing the Child to his chest, he whispered,
"O let me die or never more awake!
My crown, my kingdom,
And all my fading years for this!"

The Boy laid his soft, small hand
Against the hard old face.
A long-forgotten joy welled up inside of Melek
As he felt the little fingers
Tangle in his old white beard.

A lion moved out of the shadows.
Melek might have frozen in his fear
Except a strong euphoria now wrapped his soul.
Transfixed in reverence, he worshiped,
Fearless in the wondrous night
Between a lion and a Child.

"Melek!" the voice seemed to come
From the beast born out of the shadows.
"This Child is yours in but a while.
Hold Him that His strength may come to you as
        bread.
Aged though you are,
You yet must make a journey.
It will be long and yet
True kings must spend themselves
In ways that their nobility demands.
Kiss the Boy . . .
Then set Him down and pray for strength
To bring your crown
And follow where the stars may lead.
The Child is yours . . .
But not until tomorrow."

The old king kissed the Child a final time,
But held to Him, refusing to release the joy.
"Now," Roared the lion, "Set Him down.

We only keep what we release.
We own by letting go!"

The old man set the Child down
And watched Him toddle toward the lion.
Together they walked into the shadows
And were gone.

"But where? When?" The old man asked.
No answer came.

The garden was as deserted as it had been
Throughout the empty years.
Melek's remorse stabbed at his aching reverie.
Funeral by funeral he'd felt this pain before
Till now, at last, his family was gone
And grief was all he had.
Grief—monstrous grief:
His meat, his drink,
His mocking mirror, his cold forbidding nights,
A decade of a table set for one.
He climbed the steps again,
Leaden . . . slow. His tired old limbs
Despised their heaviness.

When finally he reached the top
He looked into the heavens.
The stars were not his friends.
They were glittering deceivers—cheating him
With bright mirages—scalding all his dreams at
        midnights.
His eyes saw stars.
His mind, the vanished lion and the Child.
Suddenly he was seeing for the first time
What he had studied all his life.
The constellation of the lion in the high night dome!
His vision turned to the Constellation of the Child.
His face lit up at once!

He flew into his study, throwing
Star charts, all unsorted, to the floor.
What a night this was!
He was old and dying
When it first began.
Then came the Child and lion
And he was young until the vision died.
Then he was old again.
"But now," he wept in joy.
"I'm young all over!"
He held a parchment chart to the torchlight.

He flung it down upon the
Heavy table in the center of the room
And grabbed a quill and rule.
He dipped the pen in ink
And traced a line between the
Two great stars of second magnitude
As they appeared within the constellation of the
    lion.
He moved the quill to the opposite side
And drew a similar line between
The brightest stars in the Constellation of the
    Child.
He then extended those two lines until
They intersected near the center of the chart.
His eyes gathered tears in glinting torchlight
As he transcepted and arced the angles.
He shook his head and cried in self-rebuke:
"Melek! Never more call yourself
The friend of stars for you have
Lived in self-pity till it obscured your science.

"Grow young, old fool, the age of dark is past!
Convergence comes! You have an heir at last."

He walked to a large glass case
And reaching in, removed a crown.

He brought it to the marble table
And threw it down.
It settled like a spinning coin
In retiring echoes through
The dark corridors of his palace.
"Tomorrow I begin a joyous trek
To give my crown where star lines intersect."

Saints are never giants
Who hoped to do God favors.
They are only souls
Whose needs took root
In shallow dust,
Becoming redwoods grown
From dandelion spores.

The maid, Trouvere, came just at dusk
When sky was giving up its red.
Alone with lyre she came.
She set the thumb screws of her instrument
And played the separate strings.
When all the notes lay sweet and resonant
Upon the sea of gold, gray sand
She strummed them all at once and sang:

"Earthmaker,
Shall I, who am nothing,
Dare to tell You how I feel?
I must . . . I love You!
Your world is all so richly made
My eye can drink too little
Of the glory it beholds.
A butterfly is melody,
A hawk, a chorus of delight.
A tern against the blue
Sets free an entire symphony at night.
Is all of this for me?
The sand, the stars, the purple
Mountains gnawing at the fading sun
With jagged teeth of splendor?
O stop the seep of beauty
Now flowing into me or I shall burst,
Overfilled with ecstasy.

"O, Father Spirit,
I'm in love with You! In love!
How shall I speak?
I'm only poor Trouvere."

She laid aside the lyre
And growing silent, fell forward in the sand.
"O Father, Father!

I, orphan of the dark, can
Bear no sweeter word than this!
My song is far too small a trinket
To lay before Your splendor.
O how I need You!
My passions all are spirit-kindled.
I find no purpose in such
Trivial affections that some
Have named romance.
Your Holy flame makes small
The love of mortal hearts.
In such a fickle world
To try and name what earthly values matter most
Is but a fool's pursuit."

"I crave a love that will not let me go
When it has come to know me well.
I need a love so everlasting
It holds no course with unsure human promises.
I need You, O everlasting king!
If I may be of use to You
Then call me not Trouvere
But name me only by that need You have.
Make me a cup to bear Your drink,
A salver for Your meat,
Warmth for You if gods know cold,
A path for You, if gods need feet!
Whatever meager thing You ask,
Shall be my dignity.
Call me vessel unto honor.
Then I will not have breathed Your air in vain
Nor burdened Terra with a search
To find out why I lived."

Subdued by love
She noticed not that in the darkness
There passed behind her quietly
A Child and lion.

The stealthy beast looked with blazing eyes
Made warm with desert fire.
The Child spoke audibly a single word
Too softly for her searching soul to hear.
That word was "Mother," uttered infant clear.

In any desert, water may flow sweet—
Springing up in sandal prints of
     wounded feet.

IV

The Artisan laid down his chisel
And turned to see Trouvere standing in the
     doorway of his shop.
"I'm glad you came, Trouvere."

He walked to her and took her hand
And they moved out into the early dusk.
"I'd hoped you'd come
And bring some resolution to my need.
Trouvere, we must decide
For time, like life itself, runs past us.
Will you marry me?
Please . . . I must know.
So often I have asked.
As long have you refused . . ."
He paused to cool
The urgency of issue
Lest he force her to an answer
He did *not* desire.
His urgency then melted into tenderness.
"Trouvere, I love you!"

"I wish you'd choose another word," She said.
"Let's talk of love some other time."

"Trouvere, is love an issue that can pick its time?
Can it learn the discipline of waiting?"

"O Artisan, if only you
Could understand the love I seek.
O that I understood it!
But this I swear,
There is a love not limited by lifetimes—
A noble love that shouts through the gales
Ordering brash thunderheads
To spend their roarings and begone!

And when the thunder dies
This love remains within
The conquering silence
That is the cowardly shadow of these
        retreating, whimpering storms!

"He is love—the only love which matters.
If I blot Him out, then madness rules.
But when I open up my window
Just a crack at midnight
The light of His celestial presence
Fills my room with majesty.
It's then I crave the whole of Him,
Not part or half a plate.
I must devour His love entire."
As she spoke she saw the hurt
Behind his eyes.

"Forgive me for I would not
Wound you with these words.
It's just that
My reason's eye is blinded by His nearness.
He is my treasure and my need,
A stream across the ashen wilderness
Of all my failures—
A bridge across
The chasms of my doubt."

The Artisan stopped her words and drew her close.

"Trouvere, another sort of love has brought us to
        this moment.
Can you not love both me and Him?"

He drew her even closer.
It seemed he felt her shudder in his arms.
"See," he said at last,
"Doubt hangs a heavy shadow over all our days.

Some strange and dark impending
Nudges me from sleep to fear
Like an advancing army I cannot define.
Some iron wedge like the one I sometimes use
To split a stubborn trunk of wood—
Is being driven even now between us.
Nightmares wake me
And I shake my fist into the vacant air
Above my bed and order
Leering demons from my room
As inwardly I tremble.
Love Him, but love me too!
Could He who owns the universe
Be jealous of my tiny need?
If *I* share you with Him
Can He be stingy in *His* recompense?"

He stopped and thrust at her a parcel of coarse
        cloth.
It was a loaf of bread.
Famine made his abrupt gift
An acceptable interruption
To their probing trysts of heart.

"Where did you . . ." She asked
Not finishing her question.

"Trouvere, the whole world isn't desert.
Every caravan bears treasures
And bread comes sometimes from the
        cunning.
I'd find you bread and grain to spare
If only . . ."

"It's just that it has been so long,
Since I have seen a whole loaf."
She threw herself into his arms
As though he'd given her a cask of jewels.

The desert had not yielded many treasures,
Like the loaf she held.

"They say this is the century
That Terra's sand will hold
Earthmaker's footprints."
Her statement followed nothing and preceded
        nothing.
She touched the bread and gazed out pensively.
Her eyes seemed empty as the sand.

The silence lingered, isolating in its quiet
All her wistful prophecy.

"It is theology," he said at last.
"Leave it with the temple graybeards or all its
        emptiness
Will make you empty too. Here is life . . ."
His large firm hand fell warm upon her own.
He kissed her.
She turned away and pointed to the thousand
        stars
That laughed at them as pricks of light,
Now wheedling a brilliant uproar in the
        desert sky.
"Behind those stars is life," she said.

"Trouvere, the other side of stars
Is Earthmaker's side.
This side is ours."
He left off argument.

She shrugged,
"Still, Earthmaker's not content to live so darkly
        distant
On the unseen side of any star wall.
O Artisan, do you not feel Him in the air?
His rich love richly begs my heart to sit in silence."

"But why?" he asked,
"How much silence?"

"Enough to hear the joy! The promise!
It floats around us even now.
It swims this sand in maddening intrigue
With rapture as could cleanse a world's fatigue.
Earthmaker lives! His century has come.
There shall be love enough to strike us dumb."

"Now we shall try your sweet
    communion vows
With single cup," the leper said.
"Give me your chalice first,
Then drink yourself.
But courage—for
The last three priests
Looked at my eroded face
And left their sweet religious cup
    and fled.
I later sipped their living wine—
    it tasted dead!"

V

Sand swirled across the sickly dunes!
The plague had come!
Mothers buried sons by husbands,
Lovers grieved new graves
Then walked alone.
Day by day the death carts came.
Hooded criers walked on either side
Of flat-slab wheels and moaned,
"Bring out your dead!"

Old Imperius heard their wail
As they passed by. He too was sick,
But welcomed death,
For his entire family was gone—devoured by
          plague.
He knew he soon must take *his* turn upon the
          tumbrel.
Fever gnawed at him with burning breath.
He shuddered in its wrenching spasms
As down the road the carter's cry
Grew soft with distance,
"Bring out your dead, none but the dead are free!"

He lit a candle, opened up an ancient book and
          read.

His lips moved slowly as his fevered
          eyes picked up the words.
"Blessed be the Maker of all worlds!
He saves all those who walk within the
          counsel of His love."

He paused and looked away then read—again,
"He is our help in every trial,
Watching us as eagles guard their young
In craggy nests above the storms."

Imperius' faint voice threaded
Through the weathered shutters.
"Earthmaker, I am dying, and I can bear it—
But alone?—like this?
I am not afraid of death,
But, O I am ashamed!
Human beings in times of plague,
Cast off their God-like dignity
To climb on carts of corpses."

His fever once more chilled him.

He shuddered then and fell in weakness
Knocking both his book and candle from the stand.
The falling book released a lock of golden hair.
Imperius held it to the light and cried,
"Emma, O Emma, were you ever in my life?
Am I insanely dreaming to recall
That I once held you dressed in wedding white?"

"Then we had passions, yes, and plans.
And then the years . . . the years . . . the years!
But Emma, when I held you in your final sickness
And you shuddered in those agonies I could not
        kiss away,
I cursed Earthmaker,
For my mind was webbed with hurt.
They made me lift you to the cart.
I would have buried you, my darling,
In the wild flowers of the high plateaus,
But no, it had to be in death's gray cloth!
I tried to tell myself that your death cart was the
        grand carriage of a queen.
But as it rumbled off,
I could not tell which shroud was yours.
O Emma . . . the fire came then . . . and
        now . . .
Tomorrow I will join you in the final silence.

Then Emma and Imperius shall
Be a common testament
That life's the grim report
That God is cruel and knows
No gracious news to bear mankind."

He paused a moment and
Pulled his rags about him.
"Earthmaker, are You but
The mocking, last estate of old men
Who worship healthy gods
Who've never faced the plague?"

His sickness came so hard upon him now,
He could no longer speak.
His burning fever ignited a delirium so lovely
It charmed him at the brink of death.
There stood a lion and a Child before him.

"You look too high for God, Imperius,"
The lion roared.
"He's coming unto Terra even now.
And this, Imperius, is He."
The lion nudged the Boy.
"You are wrong to think Earthmaker
Lives in realms which never can know pain.
As this Child grows He will become
A man susceptible to plague.
He, like you, will face the loneliness of dying.
And deal with all you've faced.
I give to you this promise as a gift:
You shall not die till you have met this Child."

The lion walked up to the trembling, dying man.
His giant muzzle fell full across the old and hopeless
    face.
Imperius, trembling at the lion's size,
Made one small groaning utterance.

He fell unconscious
And slept as children
Sleep on summer afternoons.
The vision died and then his fever.

But not Imperius!
He lived and read the book.
When anybody asked how he'd survived the plague
He smiled and said,
"I have one last appointment.
I dare not die till it be kept.
Convergence comes—Earthmaker learns to beg.
He'll dress in flesh to cure our world of plague."

What we know here is barely sanity.
What we own here amounts to vanity.
God sets before all men but one grand,
Worthy cup—
HOPE.

VI

Mother . . ." called a Child entreatingly.
The voice sounded as though it were just
        beyond the door
That opened on the narrow empty street.

Trouvere drew her shawl about her
And opened up the door.
Curiosity . . . drew her into dusk.
The silver light cast mauve shadows
Over purple cobblestones that wore a sheen
Of furious compulsion.
She tightened her eyes to make them see
All that might be hiding in the beckoning
        shadows.
There was nothing!

She then turned back inside,
Convinced the dusky streets
Held but the whispering echoes
Of children who had played there
In the glaring light of noon.
She lifted up the latch
To enter her small house again.

"Mother," once more came
The beckoning and plaintive word
From further down the haunted lane.
"Some Child *is* there . . ."
She thought as she walked into the night.

She reached at last the shadowed wall
And squinted into darkness.
Suddenly she saw a little form
Eclipse the bold veridian sky.
"Please wait . . ." Trouvere cried
To the shadowed blur of childhood

That hurried her to walk and then to run
In an attempt to catch the tiny silhouette.
And so she found herself
Chasing plaintive echoes
To the desert's silver edge.

"Mother . . ." finally the sound took shape!
There was a Child!
She saw Him clearly now, reaching out to her.
But as she moved toward Him He retreated.

"Please . . . I'll take You home!
Come . . . don't be afraid!"
With reluctance then the Child came forward
      slowly.
They reached out to each other
Tentatively . . . fearfully . . . hopefully,
Till at last their hands touched!
And then Trouvere picked up the Child.

"You're a long way from home, little one!"
Trouvere brushed His flaxen hair aside.

"A long . . . long way . . ."
She heard a voice behind her
And wheeled to see a man
Whose skin and clothing were as lustrous
As any gold ever mined on Terra.
She was afraid, yet the man did nothing
That would startle her.
"This Child, reality unborn,
Is your own Son . . . but not yet!
He speaks now that one word
Earthmaker must rehearse . . . Mother!"

He paused, then turned to her,
"Sit here, Trouvere,"
He gestured toward a solitary rock.

"I'll tell you of a miracle that's vast
And tiny all at once."

Trouvere sat down!
The gold-skinned man continued.
The Boy that she held
Patted her face even as he talked.

"The Father-Spirit loves with a passion
Gathered from its wide galactic essence
Out of the empty valleys of far distant worlds.
His love sweeps up its zeal from all the blazing light
Of stars, your eyes will never see.
And having gathered up the fullness of His
     universal being
He pours it now into this small
Dependent bit of flesh
That's nestled in your lap."

"Mother . . ." the Child said once again.

Ansond went on.
"Trouvere, meet Earthmaker!"

"But I don't understand!"

"It doesn't matter that you understand!
The strength of all Earthmaker's logic
Always meets the human mind as madness."

"The Father Spirit grieved the day
He closed the gates of Sanctuary
And shut the first man and woman
From the shelter of His love.
Since that day, He's known no hunger
But the one that grieves their absence.
He wants them back, Trouvere, as lovers
Of each other and Himself.

So He is coming!
Not in the regal splendor of His distant glory,
But in this small reduction that you hold!"

Trouvere was suddenly afraid.

"I'm mad!" she cried. "My love for Him
Has snatched my mind away!"
She sat the Baby on the ground and stood.
"You are not there . . . not there!" She shouted
At the Child.
The Child looked hurt.
Her heart reached out to Him.
She wished she'd not denied Him
Yet she must not weaken in her resolve
Or the world would call her mad.
She wheeled and walked away!

She turned back only once and looked.
The man, made small by distance,
Seemed to be stooping toward the Child.
Then there was no man,
Only a great beast
Whose burning feral eyes stared after her.
The lion roared.
She fled into the night.
"I must not speak a word of all I've seen
Lest He who fathers reason seem obscene."

Darkness is a cloak
That dresses imps in angel robes.

VII

The Artisan walked slowly
Through the same dark night
That had left Trouvere so troubled.
A stranger silently appeared
And walked in perfect stride beside him.

"The maid you love
Has slept with me . . ."
The villain's knife-edged words
Were out at once,
And thrust their blade of
Accusation quietly
Into his peace.

The stunned Artisan turned
And faced his love's accuser.
"What can you mean?"
He charged.
Even in the stingy light
The craftsman saw that the stranger's eyes
Were yellow-lit as if by hell.

The unwelcome intruder smirked,
"Here is the spoiling of your
Long-awaited bridal night."
He pointed to his own loins.
"Craftsman-to-be-pitied,
I have already been where you have only
Dreamed of being
When all your faithless vows are spoken.
Deluded lover!
Your maid is false as Hell itself!"

In hot and instant anger
The Artisan doubled his firm hand into a heavy fist
And thrust it forward toward the mocking eyes.

The grinning face dissolved!
His flying fist met nothing!

His fiend accuser melted.
All was silent!
The carpenter doubted first the silence,
Then his senses.

"Liar!" He shouted to the empty gloom
Where Trouvere's false accuser
Had so lately fanged the darkness.
"You've come either from my troubled mind,
Or from the gates of Hell
And I trust neither source.
All evil seeds can bear but evil fruit
When men trust demons peddling lies as truth."

"I think that God has given me a task!"
"Was the task an easy one?"
"It was and O so sweet!"
Then it was not from God,
For what He asks
Requires the rending of the soul.

VIII

A phantom hulk moved in her room!
Trouvere awoke, afraid.
A pair of eyes made luminous as glinting
      amber stared through her soul.
And yet the eyes were somehow generous
      lanterns, warmly lit.

"Who are you?" Trouvere asked.
She was answered only by the breathing
Of a beast which walked to her in darkness
And with his muzzle, nudged her from the bed.
She rose and dressed and followed.

Out, out, they moved through lane and street . . .
A woman and a lion,
Walking silently at midnight
Like innocence and power
By grace betrothed.

They came to Trouvere's desert place,
Where she had last seen
Both the Child and the lion.

The lion roared and reared himself on powerful
      haunches
And instantly became the golden man.

"Where is the Child?"
Trouvere seemed most insistent.

"There is no Child—not yet!
What you beheld was but Earthmaker's promise."

"But I held Him and He touched me and He
      spoke!"

"Majestic truths declare themselves
Before they come to be!"

At his words, Trouvere covered both her ears
And looked up to the heavens begging "*NO!*
I can no longer bear this madness!"

"Earthmaker needs a window,
An opening where Spirit may pass
With power in such abundance
That those who say
He is remote
And comfortable in sky,
May repent of their resentments.
Are you resolved to be
The window of His love?"

"Will His love be kind?"

"Kindness may seem brutal in its grace.
As when a surgeon cuts at death to offer life.
But the scars of love display
The hope that grows from pain."

The golden man went on,
"But pain does not mark only human
        suffering.
With every lesion you wear,
Earthmaker, too, will bleed,
With sky-sized wounds and agonies.
Trouvere, it is an honor to be chosen.
From all of Terra's women
This grace has come to you!
In you two very different worlds will touch
To keep each separate realm
From that poor arrogance which says,
'MY WORLD IS ALL THERE IS.'"

He gestured to the sky.
"There," he rumbled, low of voice,
"Is where Earthmaker and His Son now live.
His Son will soon walk Terra sands,
But as He now is, He cannot walk."

"And why not as He is?"

"He has no flesh and blood, and
Without these poor habiliments
He cannot stand as being
Fashioned on this planet."

"No flesh or blood!"
Trouvere voiced her brusque objections,
"How then fleshless, bloodless can He be?"

"Trouvere, Trouvere.
Let God be larger
Than your understanding!
Indeed His Son is now so vast in size
That all these distant starfields you behold
Would fit into the sparkle of His Father's eye.
Yet soon He will reduce Himself
To mortal form and size.
For greatness needs a way
To enter little worlds."

"A window?" Trouvere's mind was stretching.

"Window . . . or door . . . yes . . .
Some bridge where vastness
May change realms
And make poor Terra understand
That flesh and blood are but weak replicas
Of being in its greatest form.
His coming will overshadow you with inner life.

I've nothing more to say but 'wait' and 'yield.'
Clutch these two words unto your soul."

Ansond melted into night.
Trouvere found herself alone.
"I'm mad!" she cried,
"Earthmaker, torture me no more.
I beg You!
Do not ask this forfeiture of mind.
From such delusions can I mother God?
No! Never! Never!
The wombs beneath such troubled minds
Bear murderers not kings and gods.

"Am I too frail to hold the honor that is mine?
If infant men may bring their mothers infant woes,
What sort of pain may infant Gods produce?
I won't be vessel to immortal schemes
My weakness cannot bear such heavy dreams."

Some tribesmen still believe all lion
    cubs are stillborn
And cannot live until their sire
Breathes in their nostrils, waking them
    to life.
In such a way
Eden grows in savage souls.

IX

Trouvere dreamed and in her misty mind
She walked across a barren desert-scape
Until she met the lion.
Dropping to her knees before the beast,
With reaching hands she held his giant head
And stared into his tawny face.
A glint of starlight, like a desert diamond,
Gleamed in the beastly eye.
In that same lion's eye
She saw a mirror scene—An aged king,
Stumbling through a desert storm,
Shielding his face from cutting sands.
One of his thin arms ran through a coronet of gold
And the other ended in a hand that gathered
His hood tightly around his throat.

The old king stopped at length
And turned his back.
"As my name is Melek,
I never will be conquered;
I will live and see this Child, whose kingdom shall
Make one of two.
Whose very being shall unite all life."

He said nothing else, but turned into the wind
And walked.

Trouvere repeated the name he'd given to the
        wind,
"Melek, bear on, old one, somehow I know we'll
        meet.
Earthmaker," she said in reverence,
"Protect this patriarch."

She released the lion's head and sang
Unto the beast,

"Glint in this lion's eye, guide Melek's feet!
Illumine all his wilderness tonight.
Old kings give up their crowns reluctantly.
Dim eyes beg sight and cling to dying light."

"Do lions cry with grieving sighs that rise
As stars in lion's eyes? Take leave of me!
Hold not your place in this small ordered sea.
I give you up! Roar elsewhere and be free."

"Stalk him, great beast, lest he should ever doubt.
Roar through the winds and tempest as you may.
His ebbing mind needs find a guardian.
He'll die without a lion in the way."

The night dissolved.
Trouvere's singing folded into mist,
The fire-eyed beast was gone.

Hundreds of miles eastward across the desert
Melek struggled on against the winds.
His stamina was nearly gone.
He fell in sand that the wind
Whipped into devouring cruelty.
On his knees . . . to the wind
He felt a sudden reprieve in the deadly air,
As if some form had come between him
And the storm's ferocity.
He turned to see the lion he had first seen
In the Palace Garden.
"You are the sign," he whispered to the beast.
"We are both kings. How odd we both should
        meet.
Perhaps we'll lay our crowns at better feet."

A dying child gives life up willingly,
If he is loved and held while dying.
Triumphant innocence can smile upon
Such terrors as make gladiators scream.

X

From time to time Imperius would talk
With the small Child promised
By the golden man.
The Child existed
Only in his deepest longing.
"Dear little one . . . the world is sick.
The plague walks with heavy boots
That gouge the earth with graves.
The night my Emma died she knocked a
Jar of water to the floor,
And even as the water flowed away
Her life ebbed, too.
I studied all the shards of glass that shattered
Round her bed like broken bits of life."

"But enough! I speak but to myself,
And wait for You.
Run along now . . ."

He imagined the Boy walking off.

Thus, the Child of Promise came and went
Keeping all his loneliness at bay
Until the glorious day should come.
"O Infant Grand, I bless Your fragile coming
And before I join my Emma
I'll yet reach out to lift You to my breast
And close my life with joy.
Death, you can no longer paralyze.
The Child-God comes, till then my spirit flies."

Adam's ghost walked through
    Hiroshima's ruins
Giving apples to the dying,
Begging their forgiveness.

XI

On that same night when
The desert solstice was born
Ansond, leaving off his lion form, came once
        again.
His presence did not frighten Trouvere now,
Nor did she draw away in fear.
"All argument is gone—
I am Earthmaker's window,"
She said softly.

"And can you live with pain?"
Ansond inquired.

"I do not relish pain,
But, I shall steel myself
To bear it as I can."

Ansond smiled and vanished in a swirl of light.
The path of fire
That followed him to nothingness
Gathered itself in brilliant incandescence
That spiraled upward, reversed its course,
Then bore down as wild determined flame
Enveloping her now willing soul
And wrapping her compliance
In conceiving fire.

When Trouvere could no longer
Stand the brilliance
She fell unconscious.
Miracle and love were one at once.
Spirit-life took root in clay.
The fire passed and Trouvere slept!
And as she did, a vision
Unfolded in the dying fire.
A man and woman,

Bent by age and great despair,
Walked to her sleeping form.
The Matriarch reached down,
And touching Trouvere's hair, wept.

"You, child of yielded spirit,
Will serve Him better far than I once
    served.
I wanted knowledge, yes, and power.
I wanted disobedience to make me wise,
And thus devouring the forbidden
I changed His paradise to Hell,
And cursed the streams of Sanctuary
To call myself 'like God!'
See what a scourge is laid
Upon my disobedience.
I loved the serpent more than He
Who woke me on a summer day in Paradise."

"Don't talk this way, woman from my side!"
The old man grieved to see her crying.
"Dearest love," she said,
"You know it is true!
I cursed it all, and worse, I then cursed you.
Yes, you the most of all.
I could cry a requiem for
Sanctuary, if by my tears
I could undo the misery I've done."

"No . . . no!" he cried. "You take
Too much upon yourself."
He drew her near.
"My sin is mine . . ."
His words died.
Silence reigned.

"She is beautiful, isn't she?"
The woman said at last,

Gesturing to Trouvere, sleeping still beneath
The thinning light streams.

"She is as you are . . . beautiful!"
The old man said.

"As I *was?*"

"You are!" He insisted.
"Do you think that beauty ever lies
In youth or perfect features?
Tonight our double sin is healed.
Within this maid is Sanctuary born again."

"O Trouvere, how blessed you are!"
The woman cried exulting.
"I gave birth to quarreling sons,
Whose egotism, like my own,
Only spoiled all the earth it touched.
Reverse my ruin!
Live and give life!
Earthmaker's Son and song unsung
Is sleeping now
In this small, yet glorious space,
The world calls Blessed.
Two women are we here
Whose trust and lack of trust
Stabbed and made alive
The destiny of every soul.
Blessed, too, is He who sleeps within you!
He'll rise to smash the hated gates
I closed on human hope."

"Come away." The old man took her arm.
Drawn by her man, the woman walked
        away
With steps made light with hope.

In a final, and lingering glance,
She turned and wept,
"Live, child of earth, to bear the Child of sky.
Give Terra life that's unafraid to die."

The world lies lost without restraint
When gigolos kneel down with saints.

XII

The Artisan had made the matter firm.
The marriage date would be
In six short months—
So brief and yet so long a time!
On his way to see his maid,
The accusing stranger came again.

"Surprised to see me in the daylight?"
The hooded man rejoined.
Those were the very words
The Artisan had framed within his mind.
A rasping voice emerged from underneath the
    hood.
If words can be said to coil as serpents do,
His words came
Twisted—adder like,
"Nightly now, I'm sleeping with your maid.
Odd, isn't it, that one man's future hopes
Are but the spent reality of other men's past
    appetites.
Forbidden treats are ever best."

"Liar!" The craftsman ground the whispered word
    between his teeth.
Gurgling laughter issued
From the shaded face.

The stranger's hood was brown
But filigreed with silver threads
That twisted in metallic cobras,
Coiled, and entwined among
Emblazoned leaves of gold,
That rose from copper apples
And other kinds of pale, embroidered fruit.
The curious evil needlework
Intrigued the Artisan.

"You like the silver-threaded hood?"

The Artisan walked unanswering.
The stranger turned his head enough
To let the sunlight catch the high cheekbones
Beneath the canopy of brown brocade.
The glancing light flew upward to his eyes,
Which, like the stranger's words, seemed evil,
Slitted, old,
As though they'd yellowed
With a thousand centuries of staring hate.
The hood fell back.
The man-thing laughed, and tossed his head
In arrogance, then grinned and disappeared.

The Artisan was troubled.
His hallucinations came too often,
And seemed too real to doubt.
This hideous demon
Had twice accused his own beloved.
He trusted his Trouvere and yet . . .

"O Trouvere, Trouvere!" He said half-aloud
As he continued down the narrow lane.
"I betray you in my heart by my unwilling
Remembrance of this liar's vile eruptions."

He stopped his mumbling and tried
To walk past all his fears,
But froze as he beheld a cobra,
Black as gliding ebony, race past him.
The venomous creature stopped
At a distance in the dirt ahead.

The serpent twisted its sleek body
Into a triple circle, then
Lifting its wide head, glided quietly away.

The lovers met,
Some distance from Trouvere's small home.
"O Trouvere—I'm tormented
By visions that my mind cannot lay by.
Evil walks with me.
It interrupts my sleep
And tells me lies too hideous for you to bear!"

"Dear Artisan, I too
Am stalked by visions
Of a lion in the night."

"What can you mean a 'lion in the night'?"

"I dare not tell you
What I mean,
I must not try . . . only trust me—
Indeed let us both trust.
I'll trust the giver of my vision
And you trust me and wait."

"How long to wait to trust?"

"A little while . . . a little while . . ."

"A little while," he looked away.
Tears filled his repetition of her words.
They embraced, as somewhere in the weeds
Beside the road a reptile hissed in sighs,
Grinned over fangs and watched through jaundiced
    eyes.

They say that eighty fathoms under
    earth is Hell.
Believe it not!
It lies in shallow flesh—
Three inches underneath the chest.
There jealousy may dwell.
Dwell, nay, not merely dwell,
But writhe and sting itself to death.

XIII

When they approached the stoop
Of Trouvere's home
There lay upon a boulder there
Beside her door,
A brown cloak, sewn with silver filigree.

"Trouvere, where did you get this?"
The Artisan demanded, grabbing at the cloak.

"Nowhere. I got it nowhere.
I don't know how it got there
Nor whose it is." She rambled.

The Artisan's doubts grew fangs
As real as those that marked
The hooded being of his all-elusive foe.
He turned in silence, only for a moment,
Then wheeled and nearly shouted:
"Trouvere! My heart is torn!
I've met a man who says that he . . ."

"Yes?" She gave a single word and waited.

"This cloak . . . again . . . whose?"

This time he spoke so loudly
Her tears no longer stopped behind her eyes.
The carpenter beheld her tears,
But saw them as admission.

He threw the broadcloth to the ground.
As his anger faded to remorse,
He softened his denunciation,
"Trouvere, I never gave you cause . . ."

"O Artisan, your words are knifelike.
They swarm at me like murderous assassins.

I can't know all that troubles you,
Still I can see a gray doubt in those eyes
Which once beheld my face in love.
O beware the demon, Jealousy!
This devil wrecks the excellence of all relationships.
Jealousy's a libertine that sleeps in unclean beds
Conceiving other hungry imps that breathe
    suspicion.
He nibbles first at older promises
And then devours all future hope of
Seeing love restored.
He sometimes teaches martyrs
To despise their faith
And then delivers them
To nothing more than faithless living.
Scorn, love, his bitter doubt
Lest doubt's rehearsal
Form in you a bitter heart.
The hardest lies which we must circumvent
Are those our troubled, unsure hearts invent."

Motherhood's second heaviest burden is
That her children be compelled to watch
    her die.
Her heaviest burden is to be compelled
    to watch them die.

XIV

Trouvere's estrangement from her Artisan
Left her in sleeplessness
And set her wandering.
She heard a muffled sobbing as she
Passed a shaded section of the wall at evening.
She turned to see a woman huddled,
Weeping, with her head bent low,
Almost between her knees.
"Why do you weep?" Trouvere asked.

The woman, never looking up, replied,
"Please, go away!"
Trouvere wanted to comply, but
An aching that would not let her go
Prohibited her leaving.
She sat until the woman's grief seemed
Less violent, then she asked, "Are you alone?"
She felt ashamed to ask so obvious a question.
She was alone and her cutting grief
Further isolated her from any who might care.

The woman continued looking down,
Her tear-streaked face stared into dust.
"I have just come from the city!"
She stopped and let the silence rule.
"Yes . . . ?" Trouvere urged.

"My only son was executed there,
And I beheld him die," The woman said.
"Have you children?" The huddled being asked
The question muffled by her buried face.

"I shall have," replied Trouvere.

"I remember when my son was born . . ."
She paused again as though her frail tongue

Could not support the leaden words.
"I held him close and loved him for his helplessness
    and need.
That memory shall never leave
For today I watched him die.
No man can die a man
While any mother's there to see.
He died a little boy! A child who needed me!
And hurting were his eyes
As when he was a boy!

"He spoke but one word, 'Mother.'
His was not a man's voice,
Nor was his pain a man's pain.
He was a boy crying out to me,
Somehow as he did
When once he scraped a knee or
Felt a fishhook tear his infant hand.
I knew what to do back then.
Today I did not know."

"Executed and so publicly . . . that's the part
I barely could withstand.
His dying was so observed.
I begged the gawking world
To turn their eyes away in mercy.
For there are times when merely looking is a crime,
When our hurt should have the chance to hide
From eyes whose staring but enlarge our wounds."

"So at his dying place
I would not look at him
And add the pain of my own scrutiny."
She was silent for a moment,
Then went on.

"When he was but a little boy
I used to hold him near and think

How much he'd grown and how heavy he'd
    become
With the passing of each day.
Too soon the time came when
It grew difficult just to lift
Him into bed for naps.
Then once when we were dancing at the festival
He scooped me in his arms and held me
And I was most embarrassed.
But young men are so prone
To show the world their strength.
And yet I thought, it's right
For sons to carry parents
And hold them as a symbol.
For when he lifted me,
I saw the end of his dependence.
I knew the days would come
As surely as my years advanced;
I'd be infirm or invalid
And then my strong young son would carry me
As I had done for him."

Pausing for a moment she shrugged her shoulders
As if to escape the weight of all that she had seen.
"It was strange today when they took him from
His dying place, I leaned against his gallows
And they placed him in my arms.
I begged them do it and they did!
O he was light! I was so surprised!
I'd never held him as a man
And he was light . . . light!
I looked at him, remembering,
That long-ago dance festival.
I thought, if I could only hold him up
And dance him back to life,
I'd leave us laughing at his death.
I would unwrap the stillness

That twisted 'round his youthful smiling face
And he would live.

I held his wounded head a final time
And wept and said, 'O son!
Think not this furious turn of circumstance
Could ever turn me from the obligations of my
      motherhood.
I held you when you took your first, new breath.
I hold you now beyond all final need of breath.'
I kissed him then and called him 'sonny.'
It was not his name
And yet the name I'd always called him
When he fell asleep upon my lap.
'Sleep, sonny, for this world did not deserve your
      presence.'"

Silence!

Trouvere at last reached boldly out to her
And raised the woman's face toward her own.

The faces were identical!
The woman was herself!
Her blazing, tear-washed eyes
Cut visions like a sword through Trouvere's soul.
And as Trouvere stared into her own suffering eyes
The woman's solidarity gave way.
She melted into air leaving Trouvere
Stunned and alone.
Still reaching to her crushed, inner self,
She turned her ashen, frightened face to the sky:
"Such shadows alter hope . . . Hold time in sway.
Die now, dead eyes, lest you behold that day!"

"Look, Saint, I'm a God made warm
   by love,"
Said a devil impersonating deity.
"I believe you," cried the Saint.
"May I see the scars you spent in
   loving me?"
"I have no scars!"
"Then you're no God! Nor do
   you love!"

XV

The outside air was cool
Enough to let her fevered mind
Hold counsel with itself.
Weeks now had gone,
Her Artisan had not come.
Trouvere looked down at herself,
Convinced she could no longer hide
What she must make her world believe.
She'd once seen a woman executed for
        adultery
And the vision of the martyred woman
Would not leave her mind.
She heard again, and even yet again
The felted thumping of the stones.
Even now she felt a stinging in her eyes—
The burning heat that told her
Should she herself face such a crowd
She would not beg for life.
Still, doubts, like arrow volleys, flew at her.
Could she be mad? Could her vanished night
        of glory
Have been an hallucination of such strength
That she, herself, believed it?
Her mind seemed firm and yet she knew
That those most mad were
The last ones to suspect their madness.

"Earthmaker!" She cried. "I need You still
To separate bright reason from insanity."

Suddenly, the sky burst with a
Floating fleck of light
That doubled all its silver
Into gold and settled at her feet.

A lion roared.

"Trouvere, you are the chosen window,"
Ansond stepped out of glistening shafts of light.
"The season of your trial by fire has come.
Now you must hold to truth
While others call it false.
Friends, relatives—your only love will soon
Lament your broken mind.
Some will threaten you
With stoning and with death,
But do not fear!
You *are* Earthmaker's Chosen!"
He touched her once again,
Then lionized himself,
And leapt into invisibility.

Trouvere shouted to the sky which swallowed him.
"Earthmaker! Terra is a needy place,
I'll spend the coins of trust to purchase grace."

The lips know only shallow tunes.
The heart is where great symphonies
    are born.

XVI

Imperius would wake and wonder at his gift
    of life.
The plague that came as shrouded horror
Had now abandoned every street
And while the living were not many
Imperius rose each day to bless the sun
And remind himself that every meaningful breath
Of life was given to some purpose.
His purpose was to wait!
He waited for a Baby.
But where he and the Child would meet
Was as much a mystery
As his return from that murky land of near-death.

He still talked
With the Child he oft imagined.
Indeed his dreams were filled with children!
And thus he slept the sound sleep
Of those whose confidence was locked
Away in vaults on other worlds that
Never had known thieves or threats.

One night, however, his sleep unfolded
In a vision so majestic he woke up
In another time.
At last he understood the Glory
Of his waiting for a little Child
For he saw the man the Child would become.
The Child-made-man was tall with eyes that
    pierced the gloom.
And yet those eyes absorbed
All pain and hurt and cleaned the wounds
Of lepers just by looking on them.

The Child-made-man walked forth into the streets
And passed His shadow over thronged cities.

He passed a crumpled soul wrapped in self-pity,
Begging by a wall.
"Why do you beg?" the Child-man asked.
"I must beg to live," the beggar answered.
"My feet are only useless clubs that will
Not carry me."

"Look on Me, My name is Liberty!" the Child-man
    cried.
The beggar looked.
His useless feet were suddenly made strong.
He rose upward, steadied himself
Against the nearby wall
And then walked . . . made whole by joy!
The Child-man smiled and in that instant fell.
His feet were now just stiffened clubs
On which He could not walk.
The beggar's gnarled crutches lay yet upon the
    ground.
He now used them to pull Himself upward
And hobble slowly down the lane.
"I am Liberty," He said, "Made swift by beggar's
    crutches!"

He walked on through the dreaming mists
Of human misery until at last
He met a youth whose face was torn by scars.
Her weeping made His soul reach out.
"Why do you cry?" He asked.
"Can You not see?" she replied.
"I fell into fire when but a child and
Now my disfigurement is but
A mask of ugliness that forbids all hope
Of living in a secure world made warm with
    friendship."

"Look on Me . . . My name is Hope!" the
    Child-man commanded.

She looked and as she gazed
Her scars gradually sunk in new soft skin
But broke like ugly calluses of hate on His own face.
As her countenance became clean and young and
  beautiful
The Child-man, in that moment, was born a thing
  grotesque.
She ran off into the distance
And her joy was wondrous great
But not as great as His.
He leaned hard on His crutch and through a
Face made ugly by His own desiring
He cried after her in joy.
"I am Hope, made beautiful by craving ugliness.
I am Liberty, made swift by beggar's crutches."
He sang and hobbled slowly up a long, defiant hill.

In but a while, the Child-man came across
An old man shivering in the cold shadows of early
  evening.
He was naked and the night would soon steal his
  life.

"Have you no coat?"
The Child-man asked.

"I had one but it was stolen."

"Look on Me! My name is Love!"
He twisted from His own coat
And gave it to the man.
His giving left Him nearly naked
And unprotected in the night.
The man who had received His coat
Walked out into streets, made warm by knowing
His nights would be endurable.
The Child-man smiled!

"I am Love, made warm by nakedness.
I am Hope, made beautiful by craving ugliness.
I am Liberty, made swift by beggar's crutches."

At last His hobbling brought Him
Through a thousand sunsets and vast fields of
        misery.
He stopped and shuddered at what lay before Him.
He grimaced as He faced a distant hill.
For there He saw three gallows.
He hobbled to their center.
His eyes were filled with tears.
For on the first gallows He saw the man
Whose feet He'd taken as His own.

"Did You but make me strong to let me die?"
The dying man confronted Him.

The Child-man wept but gave no answer.

On the second gallows He saw the girl.
"My face is clean. You gave me both relationships
And friends . . . but only for an hour like this?"
The Child-man reached to her,
His eyes blinded by His pain.

On the third gallows was the
Man who owned His coat—
A coat now drenched in dying.
"Was My coat warm?" the Child-man probed.

"What is warm, Child-man?
Did You but make me warm
To face the chill of death?
We're all dying, can't You see?
All You did for us was temporary.
All Your gifts were but for our little needs.

Now we face the terror from which no one is ever
    free!
Do You not care!
We're dying . . . dying . . . dying!"

His hanging lovers all watched as He hobbled
To the center of their triple dying.
He climbed upon an empty gallows, hanged
    Himself
Until His hands and feet bore all their wounds.
Then His head collapsed
Toward the earth.
Their dying eased . . . *their* ropes came free,
Their hands and feet could move again
And they climbed down.

The Child-man smiled.
His final, precious words
Soared somehow sonnet-like:
"I am Love, made warm by nakedness.
I am Hope, made beautiful by craving ugliness!
I am Liberty, made swift by beggar's crutches!
I am Life that makes alive by dying."

Alive and free the trio walked away,
And passed a woman struggling up the hill
But paid her no attention as she climbed.
Soon she stood alone beneath the center gallows.
Her hood fell back.
The dying Child-man looked.
Their eyes met.
"I was afraid you'd come," He said.

"O Son, was the planet worth all this?"
She gestured to His hanging form.
"Should love bleed out its last for worlds
Too self-concerned to pity all its whispers
When it has lost the volume of its voice?

You loved but have no lovers.
Where are all those for whom this price is paid?"

His tears fell down to see her hurt.
Her tears fell too.
Their weeping birthed a river
Mighty in its grace.

Imperius awoke!
His face was wet!
He cried unto dark, more dark than even that
Which he had known when Emma left him,
"Should love in any world know such a fate?
Oh, glorious is this Child that I await."

Hate is bread—baked slowly
In the oven of our narcissism
And eaten with such haste
That we devour our hands,
And never notice till
We reach to touch what we adore
And find our fingers gone.

XVII

The desert sun streamed
Through the window of his
Shop at midday and
Ignited fragrant odors
From the sweet new cedar chips
That covered all the floor.
The fiend who dogged his doubts
Formed in a shaded corner
And sneered an unwelcome greeting.

"Hello, Artisan!"

The Artisan grimaced but said nothing.

"Your Trouvere is with child . . ."
The demonic voice went on,
"My child, not yours, poor unwise lover.
Will you not now call your Trouvere what she is?"

"Liar!"
Was all the Artisan could say.

"You called me liar before and found me true."

"I found your cloak beside her door.
I found my own mind subject
To discrepancies that you suggested."

"Bid the blindness in your love
Be healed.
Call hate, hate.
It is your maid who lies, not me."

"She cannot be with child.
She loves me
With a love that I return.

I see her smile, gentle as a desert rain,
In every sunrise."

"Give me no poetry
That sweetly closes both its eyes
While the unborn Child she carries,
Makes mockery of all your pretty words."

"Never!" cried the Artisan.
"I will not doubt my love's fidelity.
Doubt never cheapens love, it cheapens me.
But leave me, man . . .
I'm going now to see Trouvere.
Perhaps the months apart
Will soften our togetherness
And love will live as once it did.
But whether it live or no
She shall give answer to my doubts
And I will try your accusations
At the source of truth."

The Artisan left Trouvere's accuser.
Saying nothing else he journeyed to her
        home.
Still in his mind he wondered,
"Can Trouvere give any answers
When my very questions kill all trust?
Still, I'll ask them so I may sleep again."

Finally, he neared her simple dwelling!
She watched as he approached.

He knocked!
Trembling uncertainty at his appearance
Could not prevent her wild exuberance.
She flung the door wide.
"Artisan!" she cried,
And threw herself into happy arms

That closed about her.
His embrace seemed to say,
"Whatever is untold . . .
Whatever is withheld,
Whatever I believe or disbelieve
For this one moment of our lives, we touch,
And touching is the prize of lovers."

"They made the moment last
So that the aching weeks
That had separated them
Lost all their force.
They spoke in whispered syllables
Soft enough to heal
The hurt in all that must be said.
"Trouvere," the Artisan began,
"I know a man. And yet I don't.
He stalks me in the darkest fissures
Of my doubt.
He tells me things so damnable and dank
My heart can scarcely give them space."

"What sort of man?
What sort of things?" she asked.

"Don't think me mad, but pity me.
He says he is your lover!"

Trouvere turned away
And then turned back.
Tears stood silent in her eyes!
The Artisan felt so ashamed.
"Forgive me, dear Trouvere. I know not what to say.
But hear it all and then release my mind.
Each time he comes he says—
O forgive this blasphemy—
That you are with child—his child!"

Trouvere could bear his words no more.
She broke in weeping.
The Artisan drew her close
Begging, "Forgive me! O forgive, forgive!"
For a long while neither of them said anything.

"Artisan," she said at last.
"I too have had a visitor.
He springs from nothingness
And fills my mind with truths so overwhelming
That I scarcely can receive them all.
He told me I would have a child and—"
She stopped, knowing that
Her words defied all credibility.

"Trouvere, please . . ." he choked,
"Let's live with open hearts,
And lay it all in sun,
For nothing honest lives in shadows."

Painfully she turned her face toward him.
"He told me I would have a Child
And He would be Earthmaker's Son!"
"And you believed?"
The Artisan's voice rose to shouting level
That spoke the volume
Of his rising doubts.

"Please," Trouvere interrupted,
"You said let's lay it in the sun.
You must believe, for if you don't
I have no hope in all this world
That I shall ever be believed by anyone!
Whatever your strange visitor has told you,
He has lied!
I've never known nor yet desired another man.
But I must tell you

What I can hide no longer,
I AM WITH CHILD . . ."

The words were crushing stones.
He shook convulsively
And turned his face against the wall.

At last he turned again to her.
"Trouvere, I've never doubted anything you said.
But always in the past
I found some logic in your love.
You are for me this night
Life's great unhappiness.
If great Earthmaker be
And if He be pure love,
He would not, could not, violate
His own longstanding rules
Of nature and morality."

She broke again into tears.

He stood. She clung to him.
He pushed her back and turned,
"I'm going now, Trouvere.
While every value I have ever cherished dies.
The day has fled and left me only night.
The love is dark that once I blessed as light."

"God," I cried, "I need You,
Can You hear me? Are You there?"
The great glass throne seemed empty.
There was no one in His chair.
I waited in His absence.
Finally on my bloody knees
I laid my doubting obscene head
On His high-gilded guillotine,
And meekly said, "I trust!"

XVIII

As leaden days marched on
The crust of numbness
'Round her heart gave way.

Her singing joy subsided.
Earthmaker seemed both deaf and far away.
Ansond came not.
She made her way one noontime to the well
In the condemning light of midday.
Two women watched her making her approach
And scrutinized her, sizing her
Against some conversation
That had already passed with the other women
Of the village who had measured
Trouvere's aloofness and the reasons for it.
An older woman approached, took her hand,
Pried open Trouvere's fingers,
And dropped into her upturned palm
A stone of shining black.
Then folding Trouvere's slender hand
Around the stone of condemnation
Walked away.

Trouvere shuddered.
Soon, now, she would be dragged
Into the village center
To face a world of friends
Made alien by her obedience to
Demands they could not understand.
She sat down sighing in her loneliness.
"Will no one believe me!"

"I believe you!" Said a handsome man
Who settled next to her.
"At least I want to,
But consider this:

Is it possible that in some moment
Your mind has hidden from yourself
You slept with someone . . .
Your Artisan . . . or some soldier
From the garrison nearby?
They say these foreign devils
Have hypnotic charms that drug
All those that they seduce
Forbidding remembrance
Of their every full consent.
And so you sinned and yet you didn't.
Some dread narcotic enemy
Stole chastity and left you sinned against."

Her heart resisted!
"No!" She hesitated.
"Ansond told me I would bear a Son."

"Ansond!" He interrupted!
"O Trouvere,
He's the very sort of hypnotist
That I was speaking of.
Ansond has left a field of spoiled lovers
Maimed by his hypnosis.
And did he tell you too,
That you were specially favored?"

Trouvere felt ashamed.
"Yes, those were his words!"

"Would Earthmaker give you shame
Or call such visitors His friend?"

"But I saw a towering light
Falling in cascades of incandescence."

"Poor girl. So naive! So innocent!
Light and incandescence

Are but explosions of raw lust.
Seduction makes its own starbursts
Then names them after God.
Which cults are popular
That do not feed desire?
They each one teach us
That their lusty lights have come from the
        Almighty.
Which pagan temples
Do not think their passions pure?
Which cultic prostitutes
Do not believe they do great service?
Every profane bed
Boasts some loving chastity.
Your lights were bright deceptions.
But do not call your dark hallucinations, honest
        visions.
You were the naive pawn of great hypnotic power!"

She buried her head in her hands,
And then looked up to find him gone.
She felt her soul locked in a vise
Beyond all possibility of liberation.
"Earthmaker, give me a song
That I may give it back to You.

"Send soon the gentle rain and kiss
The parched philosophies of earth.
And wash my shabby rags of trust
And clothe me with a new cleansed worth.

"Immaculate in nature come
Swab dying from my dead hereafter.
Cut healing into stabbing woe
And bind my pain with laughter.

"Send soon the gentle rain. Rich dress
The desert night with wedding flowers

And run anemones into
A bridal quilt with tender showers.

"You, Father, I adore—for You
Alone can make my madness sane.
Embrace my need or I must die.
Great Sovereign, send Your gentle rain."

Lust in final form spends everything
To purchase headstones.
All passions die in graveyards.

XIX

The serpent came at sunset,
Black as the night that beckons death.

"I know you, fiend!"
The Artisan cried.
"Night made you rank,
As that dank canyon of the damned
Where you, no doubt,
Keep your hellish nest."

"Poor Artisan, you were deceived!
Your love now stumbles through the desert,
Weeping in her childish pain.
Alone in her naiveté,
Such a pity! Such a glory!
So easily deceived, so easily confused.
And you're so like her, man!
Whose child does Trouvere carry, Artisan?"

"I cannot say, but, now, at last
I know it isn't yours.
Nor have *you* ever entered
Into my domain of promise.
Nobility is smudged so easily in fallen worlds.
My poor Trouvere but lost her way
In some betraying moment
Where innocence could be abused."

"Don't justify her infidelity and call it love.
I stung her to unconsciousness,
And in my powerful and seducing form
I lay with her."
The great snake hissed and rose,
Lowered, throwing back his head
As though he'd thrust it forward in a strike.
The craftsman grabbed a heavy wedge of wood

And cried aloud,
"Come, you ugly terror!"

The hooded head swayed forward!
The hard black lips
Wrinkled backward into a hideous smile.
And while the cobra did not laugh,
Laughter—fiendish, hellish—
Broke in the air about them
As he slithered from the room.

The Artisan was now alone.
"O Trouvere, wherever are you now?" he cried.
"I need your touch and two mere words to live—
Give back my soul and whisper, 'I forgive'!"

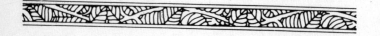

I never have believed that love is blind
And yet, I know it does see best at night.

XX

The Artisan now knew that he must find
    Trouvere.
Nor could he wait for morning.
Driven by his need for her
He moved across the desert.
Even as he walked
His loneliness diminished.
While no one visible was there,
A set of footprints fell beside his own,
Blazing shadowy depressions in the starlit sand.

Gradually the unseen traveler materialized and
    spoke:
"Artisan, Trouvere's unborn Child
Will be Earthmaker's Son!"
The words were out at once.

"No!" The Artisan replied.
"That is Trouvere's tale,
But too preposterous.
Even if such a thing were possible
Earthmaker is too kind and loving
To lay such weight on her."

"Burdens have a way
Of being heavy in every world.
Do you suppose that only humans cry?
All that crushes human spirit
Also leaves the heart
Of Universal Spirit in a vise."

The Artisan said nothing.

"Earthmaker's burden
Now passes on to you.
You, Artisan, like your Trouvere, are chosen.

And from the double weight of His favor
Earthmaker's Troubadour shall come.
Marry Trouvere and protect her,
Knowing that the Child she soon brings forth
Is not your Child.
But you were born to be the Artisan Protector.
Serve the Father Spirit
By waiting with Trouvere until the Child is here.
And remember this,
All that makes you grieve today
Will in tomorrow's world break forth as song."

So saying Ansond vanished.
The Artisan was left alone
With that slow and certain light
That issues from a new-lit soul.
He knew that in the darkness out ahead
Awaited life and his Trouvere.
And he felt lighter than he had in years,
His heaviness all washed away by tears.

When lovers meet
On wounded feet
They hurt but
Find their aching sweet.

XXI

Trouvere rose quickly—her body large with life.
She studied the night sands
That stretched in tones of mottled brown
Unto the sky-lipped desert edge.
Her eyes greeted a distant shadow.

Trouvere studied a lonely form far out against the
    sand.
Until her eyes could comprehend the joyous truth,
"My Artisan, you've come!"

She threw open the door.
Her feet kept faith with what she saw.
She ran to him!

His searching eyes had seen her too.
His leaden steps found stamina!
With hearts, so long estranged
Compulsively they contemplated joy,
Then flew toward each other's arms.

"Trouvere . . ." was all he said.
The word was signal to their need.
They met . . . a blur of grand encirclement.

A lion roared! His presence blessed
The lovers' new communion.

It was a night when many journeys ended.
Later that same night
Melek also heard the lion roar!
Imperius, too!
That night, at last, the old ones met.

The beast's voice like a living trumpet
Called them both together, certain in their
    purposes

And yet uncertain why their
Odysseys had ended
At a common time and place.

"I'm Melek," said the old king.
"And I Imperius," the plague-survivor said.
The lion wandered off
And left the two sojourners
Face to face in starlight.
After silence Imperius asked at last,
"You've seen the Child?"
"I have," replied the king.
"I've seen Him twice before and seek Him even now,
To lay before Him my old coronet—
The single legacy of my decaying realm—
A crown befitting a far better Kingdom."

"I've nothing for Him," said Imperius,
"Except a blessing.
But bless this Child, I shall.
For every night is preface to some light
Each tyranny will yield at last to right."

In self-defense
The infant Hercules once strangled
    snakes around his cradle.
But motherhood defends her cradle with
Hands made iron by love
To save a life
More worthy than her own.

XXII

Trouvere knew the time had come.
She snuggled to her Artisan
And felt his warmth.
But the warmth was not for long.
A chill passed through their tiny dwelling,
The blast of icy air awakened her.
"He's here!"

Her Artisan woke with a start.
He too felt the coldness in the air.

"Trouvere, stay here,"
He whispered as he rose
And stood on the cold floor.
Her hand reached out for his
And pulled him back.
"I'll go," she whispered firmly.

She stood and sifted darkness
With her eyes.
"Where is he?" The craftsman asked.

"We have only to ask what would be
His greatest slur," she replied.
Their eyes both turned at once toward the cradle
Where a dingy luminescence issued forth.

Trouvere and her Artisan both knew
The ugly source of blighted light.
"Are you afraid?" The Artisan asked.

"Yes, she is afraid," an evil laughter emanated
From the center of the thin light.

Trouvere, steeled with purpose,
Crossed the earthen floor

And thrust her hand into the sickly light.
She clutched the scaly head, so large and flat
Her hand could barely grasp it.
With strength she did not know she had,
She drew the heavy thing of hate
With a lashing, writhing motion
Out into the room.
She hurled the heavy body to the floor
And with her bare foot crushed the ugly reptile's
    head.
It was over in an instant, that left her marveling
That she had dared to do it.
Still the yellow glare was gone
And triumphant starlight sifted through the
    windows,
And fell upon the long, still form.

The Artisan now lit a lamp and in the better light
They both beheld the fiend's forbidding size.
Only then did Trouvere start to tremble,
For in the light, her courage seemed much poorer
Than the richness of her deed.

The snake was dead!
The room was somehow warmer.
The craftsman lifted up the lifeless thing,
Resolved to take it so far away that Trouvere
Would never have to look at it again.
He bore his evil burden out into the night.
But as he carried it, it grew lighter.
At first he thought that he imagined it,
But in a while knew that it was true.
In fifty steps across the desert
The serpent's form was fading
Even as the weight grew lighter.
In but a few steps more the snake was gone.
The Artisan now carried nothing,
And as the dead thing vanished in his hands,

He saw a hooded man running off into the night.
He shuddered at the strange event,
Chilled of soul and terrified by the knowledge
That Hell yet stalked the world.
Disappointed that the monster lived, he turned
And made his way back to the house.

"He is not dead, is he?" Trouvere guessed.

"No," said the Artisan,
"Still he has tasted our resolve
And he knows that we are settled in our
        commitment to the Father Spirit.
He nevermore shall make us sleep in fear.
For he only dares to raise his fanged face
Against those souls
Who live without a sense of who they are."
He paused a moment and then said suddenly,
"Trouvere . . . you acted with such strong
        resolve . . .
A mother's instinct?"

"Perhaps!
But more than that, I know
Our Son must one day face his hideous, hissing
        form.
Somehow, ahead of time I acted
As example for our unborn Son,
That evil cannot stand if good is unafraid."

The Artisan drew Trouvere close.
"Strength is the crown of queens who face their
        fears
And courage steels the eye, forbidding tears."

No shot was ever heard around the
    world.
In fact, in all of human history
Only two sounds have been heard
    around the entire world . . .
The first:
A newborn baby's cry, saying, "It is
    begun."
The second:
A young man's dying cry, saying,
    "It is finished."

XXIII

A knock fell firmly, gently on the door.
The Artisan opened it
With only sand and starlight answering.
Then suddenly, like an apparition
An old woman appeared,
"I am Gerain,
I know not how to tell you why I am here.
I woke as one who slept for centuries
Then came awake, called to redeem my very life
By being midwife to the purposes of God.
I tell you I am mad with mystery.
A lion roared and woke me, I followed, and . . ."

"Say no more," the Artisan reached out.

"See the heavens," the old woman's skyward gaze
        turned every face.
"Behold the stars that form the constellation of the
        lion
Have aligned themselves
Like stellar soldiers in an honor guard."

"How can this be?" Trouvere inquired.
Gerain, the old one, spoke low.
"The children in the mountains say
That when the Troubadour
Has come to sing His song,
The very stars will be as stepping stones
Between eternal realms."

Trouvere felt the Baby move within her.

Pain sometimes needs a silent witness.
And so Gerain said nothing else
But worked in quiet tenderness
While Trouvere's Artisan stood praying

As a sentinel might pray,
Looking through the very walls
As if some icon of Earthmaker was
Emblazoned past the ceiling in images
That held themselves from every eye
But his.
Trouvere knew pain but
Never once cried out.
At that small space where
The deepness of the night begins to fade
And the timid morning
Has not as yet declared itself
A Baby cried.

"There are two men at the door,"
The Artisan called through his joy.
Gerain opened the door and admitted
Melek and Imperius,
Who entered the small house reluctantly.
For there was in that room a sweet forbidding
        sanctity
That seemed to hold them back.
But Trouvere's demeanor put them so at ease
They overcame their hesitance
And pushed on in to see the Baby.

"Convergence comes," said Melek,
"The stars align themselves,
This Child is He
Whom every world has sung."

Trouvere sat upright in her bed
And in spite of every instinct
Given her by instant motherhood
She handed old Imperius her Child.

He took the Baby!
Tears came! Yet he looked past the Child,

As though his eye had focused somewhere past
    the candle flame
And fallen on his beloved,
Waiting in another world.

"Emma," he breathed, "I hold the earnest of our
    promise in my hands.
This child shall pave the way between
Our realms. The plague has fled,
And death itself is dead.
The dawn of hope is here.
Awake, ten thousand galaxies!
Polaris, bow your head! And Vega! Betelgeuse!
The vast Earthmaker, cosmic in His Grace,
Has locked Himself within a little space.
Behold, He whimpers weakly in a world
He made in strength. He who owns all lands
Is now reduced to poverty. He cannot walk
Who strode the galaxies. His tiny hands
Once light-years wide, are chubby-fingered now.
His dying world was weeping in the night.
He would not let it languish without light!
You sluggish quasars cease your cosmic flight
And listen! Here is a symphony of worth.
Oh, you proud skies, kneel down and kiss the
    earth!"

Imperius stopped his psalm and held the Child
Close to the candle fire.
He spoke again but not unto the Child,
"O Emma,
Come catch the glory etched in candlelight.
All universal being has, this night,
Broken forth in long-awaited rhapsody,
A maiden's song has spawned a symphony."

He left off speaking to his Emma
And kissed the Child.

He then began again,
"I once scorned ev'ry fearful thought of death,
When it was but the end of pulse and breath,
But now my eyes have seen that past the pain
There is a world that's waiting to be claimed.
Earthmaker, Holy, let me now depart,
For living's such a temporary art.
And dying is but getting dressed for God,
Our graves are merely doorways cut in sod."

It is faith that lights the eye—
Not reason!

XXIV

When He was old enough to walk
Trouvere brought the
Child back to the desert.
He grew, well nurtured by her love.
She told Him of His coming often
But only when He slept.
She sang to Him of love and mystery
As lullabies to keep her memories alive.

One balmy summer eve she left her Artisan alone
And carried her Son asleep within her arms
To that same desert edge
Where He had been conceived
And smiling down upon her sleeping Son she
        said,
"I met You here before I gave You birth.
There was a lion in our world then,
I haven't seen him since You came.
Old Melek, too, has left our world
Returning to his kingdom.
Our very lives are testament to his great gift.
We spent his crown for bread."

She hushed her whispered words
And traded them for a magnificat
Which bathed her sleeping Son
With a richness amplified by desert breezes.

"Did ever earth hold dreams more mad than
        mine!
That I, a desert dweller, should become
The intersection of two realms of time,
And strike the empty, sluggish ages dumb.
How shall I sing and what? Or should I sing
At all? It is too excellent for me.
If I had hushed my inner symphonies,

His music would have burst from rocks
    and trees."

"O come with me, poor world of songless men.
A storm of love has gathered in the sky
Above your heads! It shall not come again!
Run to the center of the storm: there lie!
For there at reason's edge all glory lies.
Nay, lies no longer now, but reaching comes,
Treading down the unbelieving skies,
Crushing distant ice and dying suns.

"Stare outward, starward—far as vision may.
Where eye at last meets dim capacity
And lifting night folds into dark'ning day
And stars flee from their erring galaxies.
Can spirit live in flesh? Can all that is
Not touchable be touched . . . the silent rhyme
Be heard . . . the hidden ever seen? Yes! His
Vast timelessness falls now in love with time.

"Despair at last has felt the heel of light
For love has come and plans to spend the night."

A lion roared!

The sound seemed faint and far away
Like Melek's aging kingdom.
It was the last time Trouvere ever heard the beast
And yet his roarings never grew so faint
Their glad reverberations ceased to echo in her
    heart.
The villagers told tales
Of a great lion that sometimes slept
Upon the grave of old Imperius,
Who had gone to join his Emma
Soon after he had held the promised Child.
Trouvere never doubted

That their reunion made the heavens
Sweeter than they might have been.

The seasons of all visions lose themselves
At last in ordinary years,
And in the passing of those years
The Child grew up in common ways
And all things seemed more ordinary.
And yet Trouvere could tell the age was different.
A strange, dim melody nightly came
And floated to the desert floor to kiss the sand,
As though the world had come to love itself.
Oftentimes Trouvere could hear the music
Faint and nearly voiceless. Hauntingly
It begged her wait until the Child grew.
She knew that when the Child was grown
The lion would be back and when he roared
A kingless world would welcome its new Lord.